MORTAL

BOOK 6

IN THE

SOUL GUARDIANS SERIES

KIM RICHARDSON

AWARD-WINNING AUTHOR OF *MARKED*

Mortal, Soul Guardians Book 6

Copyright © 2013 by Kim Richardson

Edited by Grenfell Featherstone

www.kimrichardsonbooks.com

ISBN-13: 978-1483982083

ISBN-10: 1483982084

Fourth Edition

More books by Kim Richardson

SOUL GUARDIANS SERIES

Marked Book # 1

Elemental Book # 2

Horizon Book # 3

Netherworld Book # 4

Seirs Book # 5

Mortal Book # 6

Reapers # 7

Seals Book # 8

MYSTICS SERIES

The Seventh Sense Book # 1

The Alpha Nation Book # 2

The Nexus Book # 3

DIVIDED REALMS

Steel Maiden Book # 1

For Cicely,

for all those great memories

MORTAL

SOUL GUARDIANS BOOK 6

KIM RICHARDSON

CHAPTER 1

CURFEW

KARA SAT ON THE edge of the bed and watched as beads of sweat glistened on her mother's forehead. She hoped the fever had reached its peak. She leaned forward and pressed a cool cloth over her mother's forehead. Her skin was pasty and sickly-grey, like a day-old corpse. Her lips twitched in her uneasy sleep, but she didn't wake up. Kara watched her mother slipping away, and she feared the worst. Her eyes stung and tears rolled freely down her face.

"It's just the flu virus," the doctors had said, "nothing to do but rest and wait it out."

They had pushed Kara and her mother out of the local clinic and locked the doors behind them.

That was three weeks ago, and her mother was getting worse.

It wasn't just a normal flu virus, Kara was certain of that. Her mother hadn't woken this morning, and it was now early in the night—it was almost as though she were in a coma. Whatever it was, she could see her mother was struggling against it. Something was definitely wrong.

A pale sliver of light poked through a gap in the curtains, and her mother's pale face glowed white in the darkness. The small room was lit dimly by the single tiffany lamp that sat on the bedside table. Like all the rest of the furniture in the apartment, it had belonged to her grandmother. Kara took comfort from their familiarity. She reached out and clasped her mother's hand—it was ice cold.

She wiped the tears from her face and glanced out the window.

Snow brushed gently against the glass. The heavy darkness outside sucked all the happiness out of her. The winds intensified and drummed along to her heart's rhythm. She felt like she was having an anxiety attack. She let out a long shaky breath as she tried to calm herself. Gently, she let go of her mother's hand.

She picked up her cell phone on the wooden bedside table.

No new calls.

The cell phone felt unnaturally heavy in her hand, like a bucket of paint. She placed it back on the small table, before it slipped from her sweaty fingers. She felt uneasy.

David was the closest thing she had to a family, beside her mother, and she needed him with her now. But where was he? It wasn't like him not to return her calls. Had he gotten sick, too? Kara fought to control the panic that rose in her chest and wiped her clammy palms on her jeans.

But what if something else entirely had gotten to David?

Goosebumps pebbled her skin as black shapes haunted her again. Darkness had always seemed to follow her, and as time had worn on, she had begun to see more and more unexplainable things, just as her mother had done. Kara saw creatures from nightmares creep from the shadows. More than once she had the distinct impression that foul beings, not of this world, had tried to attack her on her way home from her night classes. She had never shared her fears with David; she was sure he'd think she was crazy. But she knew that whatever abnormalities her mother suffered from had been passed on to her. It was in her blood. And she wouldn't risk losing David's friendship by telling him she could see monsters.

Kara sighed and turned her attention back to her mother. Her face was contorted in pain, and then she started to shake. A lump formed in Kara's throat. She had to do something. The least she could do was find something to help relieve the pain; she couldn't just sit and watch her mother suffer. There was a twenty-four hour drugstore two blocks away.

She rose from the bed—something passed over her mother's face like a shadow.

Bright green markings appeared along her mother's forehead and the side of her face like glowing tattoos. They were like words, but Kara couldn't make sense of them. What were they? She had never heard of a virus that caused markings on the skin. What was happening? She leaned closer for a better look—

Knock. Knock!

With her heart in her throat, Kara whirled around and strained to listen. The sound had come from the apartment's front door.

David! Thank God!

Kara sprinted into the hallway and made her way to the front door.

Two police officers stood on the threshold.

The woman was a head taller than Kara. She had cold calculating eyes and the pinched expression of a schoolteacher about to scold. Her long black hair was pulled back into a ponytail behind her navy-blue cap. She clutched a stack of papers and a note pad importantly.

Her partner looked like a linebacker, ready to charge. Nearly as thick as he was tall, his muscular shoulders bulged under his navy-blue patrol uniform.

Snow melted off their black polished boots and left a watery trail down the hallway.

Kara exhaled when she realized she was still holding her breath and forced a smile. "Can I help you?"

She hoped they couldn't hear the disappointment in her voice.

The woman's brown eyes sparkled, and she smiled at Kara. "My name is Officer Norman, and this is Officer Baker. Are your parents home?"

She looked over Kara's shoulder.

Kara studied the police officers' faces for a moment before answering. "Yes. But it's just me and my mom."

"Can we speak to her?" asked Officer Norman.

Kara felt tightness in her throat. "Uh...no. She's not well, you see. She's...she's...sick." Her voice cracked. She saw fear flash in officer Norman's eyes, for just a second, long enough to see it.

"What is it that you want?"

Officer Norman scribbled something on her notepad, and then she looked up. "We're patrolling the neighborhoods tonight. Making sure everything's in order."

Kara shifted her weight. She didn't like the way they were staring at her.

"Why are you patrolling the neighborhoods? Is there something wrong?"

The two officers exchanged a look.

"What's going on?"

Officer Baker looked familiar to Kara, but she couldn't recall where she had seen him before. Was he a bus driver?

"We're asking everyone to stay inside. We need to know where you are, and that you are safe, ma'am."

Kara didn't like the sound of this at all.

"Why do you need to know where I am? Is this a curfew...seriously? It's the common cold! I doubt a curfew is going to solve anything. Is there something else you're not telling me?"

From their edgy expressions, she got the unmistakable feeling that something more was going on.

"We just want to avoid more people getting sick, that's all," said Officer Baker.

His voice was hoarse as though he had never used it before. He measured Kara from under his cap, and she could see the tightness around his mouth. His aftershave was so strong that she thought he must have applied it to cover up some other nasty odor. She forced herself not to grimace.

"In the meantime," he continued, "you stay home and look after your mother. They'll find a cure and then things will get back to normal."

A cure? What were they not telling her?

The glowing symbols on her mother's forehead weren't normal. Something was terribly wrong.

Kara's fingernails dug into her palms. "My mother's in pain, she needs medication. I just need to step out for a few minutes and go to the drugstore—"

"You're not going anywhere tonight." Officer Baker pointed a large finger at Kara. "You understand me, kid? Don't think of doing anything stupid. Nobody out after seven o'clock. Those are the rules."

Kara's lips trembled. Nobody called her stupid— and she didn't care for rules. As her temper rose, so did her voice. "But my mother needs help. I'm going to get her some meds—"

"No you're not. There's nothing you can do to help her now. You stay put, you hear me?" said Officer Baker.

Kara glowered at them. She felt her hatred rise from the top of her head like steam from a pot. "Fine. Whatever. Officers."

Officer Norman shared a sidelong glance with her partner before turning back to Kara.

"Good, so we're clear. We have to keep moving, we have a lot of ground to cover tonight. Lock the door once we're gone—"

Kara slammed the door in their faces. She didn't need to be told twice. She wasn't even sure that they were real police officers. She waited until she heard the sound of their heavy boots tapering away before she kicked the door with her foot. She felt nauseated, but she knew what she had to do.

Kara dashed across the hallway and made her way towards the living room's large bay window. She peered through the plastic white horizontal blinds, her nose inches from the glass. Below, the streets were covered in blankets of white. Street lamps cast tiny yellow lights that sparkled in the snow. Headlights illuminated the street for a second, and Kara saw a black cat scurry under a parked car. Two shapes emerged from below, and she watched them make their way towards the next building to her left. She smiled when they disappeared inside.

Her mother needed meds. And no curfew was going to stop her from getting them.

"I'll show them the meaning of *stupid*."

Kara ran into her room and pulled open her closet doors. After rummaging inside, she withdrew a black winter sky jacket with a faux-fur lined hood and pulled it on. Then she grabbed her backpack and stuffed wool mitts into her pockets. She ran back to her mother's bedroom and grabbed her cell phone. Her mother's forehead glowed sporadically with toxic green symbols that looked almost as though they were breathing.

Kara bent over and kissed her mother's cheek. "I love you mom. I'm going to the drugstore. I'll be back soon. I'm going to make you better again, I promise."

Her mother didn't show any signs that she had understood, and Kara's eyes burned as she ran to the kitchen.

She grabbed the flashlight from the cabinet above the fridge and then dashed towards the apartment's front door. She pulled open the door and locked it behind her with a *click*.

Her backpack bounced against her back as she rushed down the hall, and she jumped down the stairs two at a time. The lobby was a blur of beige and brown. Once she had emerged through the glass doors, Kara was glad of the cool December air that soothed her hot face.

She caught her breath. The wind swirled around her as she stood facing the darkness. Thick snowflakes fell from the black sky like leaves from a tree. She looked over to her left. The police officers were still inside the apartment building. Snow lifted off the ground and twisted around in white whirlwinds. It was unusually quiet for a Friday night—nobody was on the streets.

The decrepit street lamps gave off just enough light for Kara to recognize the snow-covered sidewalks. The local drugstore was just two blocks away.

She would run it.

As she ran, her breath escaped her lips in rolling coils of white mist. She hurried up the quiet street, but her tread crunched against the packed snow and echoed around her too loudly.

She heard muffled voices in the darkness and threw herself down behind a parked car. Her knees stung with pain as she grazed them against the sharp edge of its rusty bumper.

Two more police officers emerged around the street corner. They walked towards her. She cursed softly and crawled around to the other side of the car. Kneeling, she watched their boots make their way past her hiding place and then disappear down the next block. She stood up slowly. Both her knees throbbed in pain. She pressed her fingers against them, her jeans were torn, and she could feel wetness on her fingertips.

Too late to go back home for some *Band-Aids*—besides; it was only a little scrape. Kara made her way around the car and back onto the sidewalk.

Something moved in the corner of her eye.

Kara froze. She peered into darkness that stared back at her. Was the night playing with her mind? Had she imaged a tall shape gliding across the street up ahead?

She turned to see a green mist pour into the street toward her like a great wave. It flowed above the snow, moving fast, against the wind. What is that? Kara shook her head and ran into the dark snowy wind. The drugstore was just ahead. The police would never see her in this blizzard.

SMACK!

Kara stumbled backwards and nearly fell. She steadied herself, blinked through her snow-caked lashes and looked up. She had crashed into someone. At first she panicked thinking it was a police officer, but she quickly recovered when she saw the girl's face.

"Sabrina?" said Kara. The young girl from first floor in her building was shivering.

"Oh my god, where's your coat? Why are you out here in the cold in a t-shirt? You'll catch your death out here."

Snow clung to Sabrina's hair like thick icicles. Melted snowflakes dripped from her nose. She trembled uncontrollably. Her pale skin shone in the moonlight.

"There's some kind of curfew, you know. You'd better get inside before the police catch you." Kara leaned closer for a better look at her neighbor.

"Sabrina? Are you all right? You're shaking like a leaf."

Sabrina lifted her head, and Kara's blood froze. Green symbols flashed across her face—the same as her mother's. Her face was hollow and sunken like she hadn't eaten in a month. Her sad empty eyes stared as if she had lost something close to her. She reminded Kara of the living dead in the zombie-movie she had watched with David.

Sabrina's lips moved aimlessly as she brushed past Kara and walked off into the darkness.

"Sabrina!"

The girl disappeared. Kara knew she could do nothing to help her.

Straining through the blizzard, Kara scanned the street up ahead. There was nothing there, but she couldn't shake the strange feeling that she was being watched.

And then she saw it.

On the other side of the street, something massive and slippery glided towards her. For a moment a street lamp illuminated the raw blood-red flesh of its twisted body. It looked like a cross between a skinned gorilla and a giant beetle, with glassy red eyes and a gaping maw.

The wind carried a putrid smell, like a mixture of vomit and decaying flesh. The snow around the creature melted away from its heat. It suddenly moved towards her. She dared not breathe.

With a giant leap, the creature came at her, thrashing massive clawed hands.

Kara tripped and fell hard on the ground. She pulled off her mitts and rummaged through her backpack, madly searching for her flashlight. She clasped it in her hand and brandished it like a weapon. As strange as it was, she found courage somehow, courage enough to go down fighting this thing.

Its razor sharp claws scraped the ground as it charged. The ground vibrated, and Kara fought the urge to vomit as the putrid garbage truck smell of the creature filled the air. She looked into its red glowing eyes as it lunged.

Kara impulsively flicked the switch and pointed the light straight at the creature.

She heard a scream but couldn't tell if it was her own or the creature's.

The creature fell back shrieking horribly, and her legs exploded in burning pain, as though a bucket of acid was eating away at her flesh. She dragged herself a few feet away from the thrashing creature. She blinked away the tears from her eyes and looked upon the thing that attacked her.

Steam rolled off the creature's front and back. Its rotten flesh slid off its body in clumps, and the smell of burnt flesh made her lungs burn and her eyes water. A large open wound in the shape of a lightning bolt zigzagged across the creature's chest, exposing the red rotten flesh beneath. Even in the darkness she could make out black liquid oozing out of the large gash.

She watched the creature howl in pain as its body sizzled and popped, thrashing around on the ground over and over. The flashlight. Somehow, the light had burned the creature.

Her legs felt warm—horrified, she realized she was sitting in a puddle of her own blood. The creature had struck an artery on her leg. She was bleeding out. If she didn't get to a hospital soon, she would die...

She dragged in a single breath, then another. She choked on the smell of burning flesh. She could barely see through the layer of snow that stuck over her eyes. Then a low growl came from behind.

Kara turned the flashlight in the direction of the noise. Too late.

She soared through the air and smacked into a parked car with a sickening crack. The flashlight flew out of her hands, hit the car and landed in pieces on the ground. The light flickered for a moment and then went out.

She lay crumbled on the ground, broken. She couldn't move. She looked into the red maddened eyes that glared down at her. She thought of her mother. The beast wailed in fury. It was going to tear her apart. It raised its giant clawed arm for the kill...

A glowing red sphere flew across the night sky and hit the creature. The sphere exploded on impact like a firebomb. Instantly, the creature's body was engulfed in red light. Its ear splitting wails filled the night sky and then the red light went out and the creature vanished.

"Kara!"

A young man kneeled down beside her. His bright blue eyes glistened with concern. She had a strange feeling she'd seen his handsome face before. But it didn't matter. It was too late. She knew she was dying. She thought of her mother, waiting alone in her room. Hot tears rolled down her cheeks. Kara didn't care if she lived or died—she only wanted the pain to end.

Let it end...

"I'm so sorry, Kara, this wasn't supposed to happen. You weren't supposed to feel any pain. This is all my fault!"

As she felt her life slipping away, she looked at him more carefully. His skin glowed as though a halo surrounded him. His blond hair illuminated his head like a golden crown. Who was this stranger?

"You'll be all right soon," continued the stranger. "The guardian angel legion needs you. This is only a changeover...this isn't the end."

Kara struggled to keep her eyes open. She was hallucinating about legions of angels—a sure sign that the end was near. She felt so cold.

The stranger took her hand, and she felt a little warmth from his. She tried to speak, to ask him who he was, but her lips were like cement blocks.

"Man, you've always been a freaking demon magnet, you know. They're always looking for your soul," she heard the stranger say. "I'll never let them take you. You're safe with me now. I've got you."

As she succumbed to the darkness, her last thought was that this guy was definitely just as crazy as her mother.

And then she didn't remember anything else.

CHAPTER 2

A NEW THREAT

KARA TRIED TO AVOID the unblinking stare of the ancient primate and looked to the ornate wood panels of the elevator instead. She could see her anxious reflection in his single round monocle. He was nearly hairless, and the sparse hairs he did have were snow-white. If the elevator jerked again, he looked as if he would burst into a cloud of white dust. Even though she'd taken the ride to the fifth level in Horizon many times, the old operator always gave her the creeps.

With its rich wood panels and tan marble floors, the elevators always made her think that they belonged in some grand hotel. She traced her fingers gently along the golden-wing crests carved into the wood panels. She was shaking. She hid her trembling hands behind her back and shuddered lightly. She had abandoned her sick mother.

Kara turned towards David. "I didn't think I'd ever see the inside of this elevator again. The oracles had made it clear, my GA days were over. Don't you think it's weird that I'm back? I keep thinking I'm dreaming, and any second now I'm going to wake up and forget everything."

"You won't, 'cause you're not dreaming," said David with a hint of a smile in his voice.

He was much calmer inside the elevator. He had only just stopped apologizing for being *late* to escort her back to Horizon.

"I'm really glad you're back. Things just aren't the same without you. You're part of the legion—in a big way. Probably one of the best guardians the legion's ever had. So it's not really a surprise that you're back so soon."

He leaned over a little closer and lowered his voice. "Besides, I knew you couldn't resist my angelic-charms, my heavenly good looks. The fact is, woman, I've *supernaturalized* you."

Kara rolled her eyes and pushed David playfully. "Oh, please. Get over yourself."

She shook her head gently. "Do you even know how this is possible? I mean...I killed a mortal, remember? I broke the sacred law."

From the corner of her eye she saw the old primate lift its ancient head towards her. She forced herself not to meet his eyes.

"I wonder why they decided to reinstate me. It's not like I had everyone's vote—I was never a favorite in the legion. I'm sure most of the GAs despise me."

"You're back because the legion says you're back, that's all there is to it. Just as long as you're here with me, that's all that matters." David searched her face with his intense blue eyes.

She remembered his panic when the crystal timer had run out and she had disappeared. She remembered his pain. But they were together as GAs once again—all was well for now.

"So what did I miss since I've been gone?"

David took a moment before answering. "I don't really know...they shipped me back to my mortal self soon after you'd left. It's weird, it's like they didn't want me back either."

Kara felt a pain in her chest. She knew how much David loved his job as a guardian. This had something to do with her, she was certain of that. "That's impossible, you're a great guardian. I'm sure you're wrong, David."

"Am I? It doesn't feel like it." David's expression tightened. He pulled out his soul blade and flicked it between his fingers. "It's the only thing I'm good at—fighting demons. There's nothing for me as a mortal, no real future. I don't have any real talent like you. My parents don't have money for me for college. Well, maybe that's a good thing, I hate school anyway."

Kara wanted to say that she was there for him as a mortal, but her words died on her lips when he turned away from her. It was like being stabbed in the chest. Maybe he was right. Maybe he felt tainted by association with her. Was there something else?

She had to admit, it was great to be back. She wondered what the other GAs would think. Peter and Jenny would be on her side; she knew that, but what about the others? Would they accept her return? The guardian angel legion had been wary of her ever since they discovered her demon father and her elemental abilities. Kara was different. She would always be different. She set her jaw.

Whatever happened, she would just have to wait and see. She pushed her doubts away resolutely.

She watched David for a moment and said. "I think something bad is happening to my mom."

David edged closer to her again. "The flu virus, yeah I remember. How was she before you left?"

Kara lowered her eyes, did her best to ignore the reproving stare from the operator, and told David about the mysterious green runes on her mother's face.

David fixed his eyes on Kara. "That's some seriously freaky stuff. Never heard of glowing green tattoos on anyone's face before, what do you think it is?"

Kara dreaded to think what it might be. "The more I think about it now, the more it sounds like some demon virus. I wouldn't put it passed them, they've been very resourceful in the past."

"I think you might be right," David said. "But don't worry, whatever it is, Ariel will know."

Before Kara could answer, the elevator stopped with a loud *ting*, the doors slid open and Kara followed David out into Horizon. She was glad to put some more distance between herself and the ancient white monkey.

The Counter Demon Division looked exactly as she had remembered. Hundreds of guardian angels rushed up and down metal stairs from second and third floors or busied their fingers on keyboards as they sat at desks spread out around the giant circular room. It was like being on the bridge of a great battle ship. GAs were huddled together around holographic screens that flickered with images of major cities around the mortal world. Were they looking for demon Rifts? What other possible threats could the legion fear?

As Kara and David made their way quietly between desks with holographic screens, a silence spread across the great room. Heads lifted, and Kara could feel their stares burning the back of her head. She straightened herself and prepared to challenge them with her own stone cold look. But her expression softened as she realized they weren't the angry faces she'd expected. They were dumbfounded, speechless, with their jaws hanging open. They were in shock. They had not expected to see her again.

Kara followed David to the large round desk on a raised platform in the middle of the chamber. Their footsteps echoed around them unnaturally loudly, as though they were walking on drums. Kara couldn't wait to sit down. A dozen stone-faced angels sat around the round desk and watched Kara warily.

Then she saw Peter and Jenny, whose grins were larger than life.

Jenny jumped from her seat and wrapped her arms around Kara's neck, "I told Peter you'd be back. I told him you would. I just knew it!" Her green eyes sparkled as she let Kara go.

"Hi, Kara," said Peter.

He fumbled clumsily with a flat metal contraption on the table. "You can't imagine how happy I am to be wrong. I didn't think we'd see you again." He laughed nervously and pushed his glasses up the bridge of his nose.

"Well that's a first," said David. He smacked Peter on the shoulder, and they both started laughing.

Kara smiled at her friends. "It's nice to see things haven't changed around here."

"Jenny got reprimanded for punching another GA," blurted Peter suddenly.

"You didn't?" said Kara, looking at Jenny who shrugged with a smirk on her face.

"I don't know what he's talking about." Jenny picked at her fingernails.

Peter laughed. "It was awesome. The guy had it coming though. He was teasing her about her hair—and then *whack*! It was great!"

Kara smiled warmly, grateful to be back amongst her friends again. "I still can't believe I'm here. It still feels like a dream." She looked around the table.

The archangel Ariel sat at the end of the table. Her mocha colored skin shone under the light, making it look almost golden. She looked like a goddess who didn't want to attract too much attention. She wore a simple short-sleeved black shirt and black cargo pants. Her toffee-colored eyes measured Kara for a moment, and then she spoke.

"Welcome back, Kara Nightingale."

"Thank you," said Kara awkwardly. "It's good to be back."

She looked over to the angels sitting around the desk and smiled. None of them smiled back, so she lowered her eyes and stared at the desk instead.

"Thank you for bringing her back to us in one piece, David," said Ariel. Kara detected a little irritation in her tone.

David looked utterly abashed by the statement. "I'm offended by your tone, your supreme godliness. I promised I would get her back safely, didn't I? Which, as you see, is what I did, your royal holiness." He pressed his right hand on his chest. "I am an angel of my word, your grace."

Ariel favored him with the faintest of smiles. "We shall see." She gestured to them with her hand. "Please, sit down. We have lots to talk about."

Jenny pushed an empty chair towards Kara. David flung himself dramatically in an empty chair between Kara and Peter, who did his best not to laugh at David's theatrical performance. But Kara could see the stress on David's face. He was putting up his usual front. Under his cheeky grin, she knew he was hurt.

"Well then," began Ariel, her voice was smooth but demanded attention. She interlaced her fingers on the table. "I'm sure you have lots of questions regarding your return, Kara, and I will get to that in a minute. And from the expressions on the faces here, I can see that most of you were not expecting to see Miss Nightingale amongst us again. Your eyes do not deceive you—she *is* back. And I am very glad for it." The archangel smiled tenderly at Kara.

If Kara had any blood in her system her face would have been tomato-red. But at the same time, she felt an overwhelming gratitude towards the archangel. Being back with an archangel's approval was bound to help smooth things over for her. She looked over to David who winked at her. Typical.

But Kara's smile quickly faded. Sitting across from her was a guardian with hazel eyes and a long blond braid. She was a little older than Kara, with sharp features and a plain face. She looked as if she loathed Kara, as if she would have spat at her from across the table if Ariel hadn't been there. What was her problem?

Kara shifted uneasily in her seat and looked away.

"Although I cannot disclose to you the details of Kara's reinstatement as a guardian," Ariel continued, "rest assured it was with the best interest of this legion and honored our mandate to the mortal world. The matter was brought before the High Council, and Kara has been granted the same privileges as any member of the CDD unit."

For the first time, Kara heard the muffled discontent of the other guardians around the table. The blond girl whispered to the angels seated next to her, but Kara couldn't make out what they were saying to each other. But from the pinched and disgusted expressions on their faces it was clear to her that they were not as pleased as the archangel that she was back. The hostility edged around the great table like a sudden frost. With the exception of Jenny, Peter and David, it was clear that the other field agents were unsympathetic to her miraculous return. They all loathed her.

Ariel gave an impatient shake of her head, and her short curls bounced lightly above her head like soft springs. "It is time to put aside any petty differences you might have—and I don't care to hear them."

Ariel's voice rose dangerously. "I see only guardian angels seated before me, and I will not have any divisiveness amongst you, especially now that everyone needs to work together on this special assignment. You have all sworn the same oath, and we are all here for the exact same reason—to fight evil."

Ariel glared around the table, waiting for anyone to defy her. The guardians didn't move a muscle and so she continued.

"Once again the mortal world is in great danger and in need of our help. An ancient evil plagues the Earth and is taking innocent lives. It is a great malevolent force that moves like a tidal wave from town to town. We have been unsuccessful in our attempts to uncover its weakness and defeat it. We've already lost five teams— and we cannot afford to lose any more. Needless to say, this will be a very *challenging* assignment."

"What's the new threat?" interrupted David as he interlaced his fingers behind his head. "It sounds pretty bad. Are we talking Seirs again? Because if we are, I'd like to volunteer to be the first to give them a serious kick in the—"

Kara kicked David from under the table and glared at him. Something in Ariel's eyes told her that the archangel wasn't in the mood to have her patience tested by David's shenanigans. Grinning like a schoolboy, David laughed playfully before settling down again.

Ariel cleared her throat. "The Seirs present a constant threat, but this is something far worse than mere mortals, David. This new threat is something we haven't seen in over a century."

"The suspense is killing me," mumbled David under his breath.

Ariel looked at the faces around the table and said calmly, "This new enemy is a dark warlock."

David leaned forward on the table. "A warlock? Seriously? With the long black cloak flying on his broomstick shooting spells? Whoa! I thought they were only a myth. I used to role-play as a warlock in *Dungeons & Dragons*." He leaped from his chair and started to mimic himself riding on an imaginary broomstick. "I've always wanted to fly on a broomstick—"

"Can you shut up and let her finish," said the same blond girl that had given Kara the look of loathing. Her voice was like ice. She smiled defiantly. "Warlocks don't fly on broomsticks, stupid. But you wouldn't know that. I guess the rumors are true...you're just a pretty face with nothing between the ears, David McGowan."

David's face hardened. "Relax, *friend*. No need to get your panties in a bunch."

He sat down and crossed his arms over his chest. Kara could almost see the steam shooting from his ears. Kara felt her temper rise as well. She glared at the blond girl, and to her surprise she was not looking at David at all, but at Kara—and with the same distasteful look on her face as before.

"Enough!" Ariel hit the table with her hand, sending a great boom across the chamber. "I don't have time for your childish games. You are soldiers of Horizon, guardians of Earth—act like it. Now listen up. I will not repeat myself. Are we clear?"

Kara turned away from the girl. Why did she loathe her so much? Kara had never even seen her before. What was her problem?

"Good, now let us continue," said the archangel with a touch of venom in her voice.

Ariel's eyes darted to David for a moment. "Warlocks are masters of the demonic arts. They can summon demons as their minions, and they use an ancient evil called dark magic. A *dark* warlock can take his victim's soul and leave the body behind to die. A dark warlock is an evil trickster of the worse kind imaginable."

"Sounds like a few angels I know," whispered David so only Kara could hear. She silently prayed that he would stop. Ariel looked livid and ready to kill anyone who interrupted her again.

"Mortal souls have a unique, pure energy," explained Ariel. "When you combine the energy of many souls together—it becomes a great power—and warlocks crave power for themselves. The warlock has already begun collecting souls across North America, and soon he will plague the whole earth with his dark magic. With the energy from millions of mortal souls, he will become unstoppable. The mortal world as you know it will cease to exist. All living things will die."

Kara thought of her mother and Sabrina with the green symbols on their faces. It had to be connected. She began to grow angry.

"Archangel Ariel, the recent flu epidemic...my mother's sick...she has these green markings on her."

"She is not sick, but infected by Dark magic—her soul has been taken," said Ariel somberly. "The markings on your mother are the marks of a dark warlock. The sickness that is spreading and killing the mortals is caused by his dark magic."

Kara's expression turned sullen. "I need to get to her. She needs my help."

"There's nothing you can do for her now," said Ariel gently. "Only the death of the dark warlock will reverse the effect and save her soul. There is no other way."

Kara leaned back in her chair and tried to stretch out the tension in her back that her rage was causing. She couldn't feel her arms anymore. One thing was for sure—she was going to kill this warlock.

Ariel raised her voice. "This dark warlock has been dead for over a century. *Something* or *someone* with great knowledge of dark magic has raised him back from the dead. They have unleashed an unspeakable evil upon the mortal world."

Kara chewed her lip uncertainly. She didn't like the wavering in Ariel's voice; it was almost as though the archangel thought they couldn't defeat this guy.

"I'm sure we can defeat this dark warlock," said Kara, aware of all the eyes watching her and thankful that her voice came out strongly. "I mean...we've defeated demons before. We've been to the Netherworld, and we've faced some pretty gruesome creatures. I'm sure we can defeat one warlock?"

Kara heard murmurings around the table, but they were quickly stilled.

"He's not just any warlock, Kara," said Ariel. "He is *the* warlock, Wergoth, a creature born from darkness and skilled with dark magic. As supernatural beings, we angels have abilities beyond the mortal realm, but we do not possess magic, especially dark magic. No *ordinary* angel can defeat him."

David whistled loudly. "So that rules us out. What the heck are we doing here then? To play board games? I'd kill for a game of Dungeons & Dragons right now."

Kara screwed up her face. "I don't understand. What do you mean we can't defeat him? We have to! I have to save my mother!"

The archangel's eyes flashed ominously. "The warlock cannot be destroyed by any means we possess. Soul blades, firestones, moonstones, or any other weapons we use on demons, will not affect him. Only *magic* can defeat him."

"And how are we supposed to get magic?" asked Kara, fighting to stay calm.

"Maybe if you'd stop asking stupid questions, she would tell us," said the blond girl in a flat voice.

Kara glared at the girl across the table. She wanted to slap her for being so impertinent. Before she knew what was happening, she stood up, her hands curled into fists.

"Kara!" whispered Jenny, her eyes wide as she grabbed a hold of Kara's arm and pulled her down. She shook her head gently. "Don't. Not now. She's not worth it."

"Oh...she's worth it," whispered David. "I'd say she's *really* worth it."

A smile spread on the girl's face. "Did the *famous* Kara wish to say something to me?"

"That's enough, Ashley," said Ariel, her lips pressed into a hard line. "There's no need for that now."

Kara lowered herself back into her seat and hid her trembling hands under the table. She was surprised at her sudden outburst.

Something about that girl made her hair stand on end. She gritted her teeth and tried hard not to imagine a fight.

Ariel leaned forward. "Magic was what defeated the warlocks long ago. The angels and white witches fought side by side to destroy the last of the dark warlocks. And as the mortal world evolved, the white witches died out—and their secrets died with them."

She folded her hands in front of her. "And yet there is one who can help us. You must seek the help of an old Cornish witch who goes by the name of Olga. She is the last of the dark witches and over a century old. The legion knows that she has been dabbling in the Dark arts for many years. You will find her in the remote village of Boscastle, in Cornwall, in the United Kingdom. The old witch is skilled in necromancy. Her charms, spells and dark incantations make her the terror of the village.

"She alone holds the knowledge and the means to destroy Wergoth. Your job is to convince her to fight with us—to destroy the dark warlock once and for all."

"Why do I get the feeling it won't be easy to convince her to help us," said Kara, reading Ariel's face.

"Let's just say witches and angels haven't always been allies. In fact, they hate us."

Kara frowned. "They hate us? Why would they? What happened?"

Ariel shook her head and sighed. "It's a very long story, and we don't have time to get into it. Olga is a dark witch, which makes her extremely powerful and very dangerous. She doesn't care much for the Legion, and she despises angels. She will not be easily persuaded. In fact, she has already killed five field teams."

David and Kara shared a look.

Ariel paused and glanced around the table. "But because her magic is the only thing that can destroy the warlock, it is a risk we must take. We know the warlock plans to perform a ritual with the souls he's collected, but we are ignorant as to what kind of ritual. He will use the longest night of the year to perform this rite. We cannot allow it to happen. If he is not defeated by the winter solstice, then all the mortals whose souls he has stolen will die. Their souls will be destroyed forever."

"When's the winter solstice?" asked Kara.

"December twenty first."

Kara wanted to jump out of her seat. "But that's in three days!"

Ariel's expression was grim. "I'm sending out two of my best teams to the witch's village. Sasha, Raymond, Ling—you'll be on Ashley's team." Ariel's eyes moved across the table. "Jenny, Peter, David—you're on Kara's team."

Kara saw the relief on David's face.

"Both teams must work together and watch each other's backs. You understand me?"

Ariel focused on Kara and when she spoke next her voice was even. "And now, Kara, I must tell you specifically why you've been summoned back."

Kara squeezed her hands together under the table. Ariel's toffee-colored eyes mesmerized her, and she couldn't look away.

"This assignment needs *your* special talent, but in a very different way. The dark witch can detect angels. She can kill you in a blink of an eye, and not before she has enjoyed torturing you first."

"Sounds like fun," whispered David.

"So far, it has been impossible to seek her help without suffering causalities. Kara, we need you to approach her without her detecting that you are a guardian. Think of it as an *undercover* assignment. We believe your *elemental* part will act as a distraction. The witch will be unable to see your angel essence. Where ordinary angels have failed, we believe you will succeed."

Kara could feel the tension across the table. She started to panic. Her throat was tight, and she thought her head was about to explode. Her elemental power was still very wild and hard to control. Simply snapping her fingers wouldn't activate it; it was triggered by her emotions—and they were extremely hard to control. Her elemental power was more like a time bomb with a short fuse.

Ariel paused, as if giving Kara the time to prepare herself for the worst. "The legion has never asked another guardian what I'm about to propose to you, Kara."

Kara could feel the unease in the chamber. The field agents and GAs strained to listen.

Kara leaned forward and shook her head. "But I'm still an angel. If, like you say, she can detect angels, then surely she can detect me too? My elemental part is still only one part of me; the rest is angel. She'll be able to see right through my M-suit."

"Not if you're not wearing one." Ariel held Kara in her gaze. "You see, Kara, on this assignment, we need you to be a *mortal*."

CHAPTER 3

MEMORY PROJECTION

KARA FOLLOWED DAVID, JENNY and Peter past the thousands of anxious faces who stood in line to be sorted into their new guardian angel lives at orientation. Their voices buzzed like millions of bees as they waited in the holding chamber that was as large as ten football fields. The air was humid with a smell of the sea. Most of the newly dead that Kara passed were happy, but amongst the cheerful faces a few miserable looking souls stood out.

A young boy of about fifteen with disheveled brown hair in a black t-shirt and faded jeans nibbled on his nails. He shook as if he were about to write his final school exams and hadn't studied. Kara remembered how terrified she had been when she had died and found herself amongst thousands of dead folk for the first time. The unknown is a terrifying thing. She felt sorry for the boy, but soon he would be all right. His petty officer would take care of him, just like David had taken care of her on her first day.

Her eyes wandered over to David. Were they ever going to have a normal life together? It seemed every time they felt like they were getting somewhere as mortals, they would get called back to the GA squad. She had never truly shared her feelings with David as a mortal. It would have been so much easier if she could remember the adventures they had shared as guardians, but as mortals their relationship had to grow on its own terms. He knew she liked him, but it was much more than that. She could never bring herself to say it—the words simply died in her throat like a bad cough. What if he didn't feel the same way?

Kara felt like a fool. She was on guardian angel duty. Any kind of emotion was taboo. Her feelings towards David would have to wait. She had more pressing matters to worry about. She could see the tiniest of frowns on David's face. She could tell he was worried—and with good reason—the legion was sending her out on a suicide mission.

At first she had thought Ariel must have been joking. But Archangels never joked. The entire CDD unit had stood frozen, waiting to hear if she would dare to confront the dark witch as a mortal. She had stifled a nervous laugh and then had nodded her head.

It still felt like a dream. To be a guardian angel, you had to be an *angel*, not a *mortal*. And yet, here she was on her way to meet with an oracle who would help her prepare for this extraordinary quest.

They passed several different offices with colossal wooden doors and flashing neon signs that flickered and buzzed. A door stood ajar and Kara could see a room with papers scattered on the floor and half a dozen oracles scurrying around on their giant crystal balls.

She followed David down a hallway. Kara could feel Jenny's anxious eyes on her the whole time, but she ignored her. She didn't want anyone to know how nervous she felt. She wanted to jump out of her angel skin, get back to the mortal world and help her mother. Thinking of her mother gave her the courage she needed to keep walking.

Think of mom...

The hallway ended suddenly, and they stood in a large opening. A single door was set against the far wall in the massive space. It was like a Super-store with only one door for the main entrance. Bigger and bolder than the other doors in the orientation area, it seemed out of place.

David walked up to the door and scrutinized it. "This is it."

Kara stepped closer and examined the door. It was ancient, with half-moon scuffmarks on the front that had worn away the stain on the wood giving it a two-toned effect. There was no handle. Above a large wooden frame was a brightly lit neon sign:

Manufacture Division # 000-0001

Below the neon sign, someone had taped a note:

CAUTION, MESSY OFFICE
ENTER AT YOUR OWN RISK!

"Sounds like my old bedroom," said Jenny. "I used to drive my mom crazy with my clothes lying all over the floor. She was such a neat freak. I told her I was expressing myself." She twirled on the spot. Her purple hair sparkled against the neon lights, and Kara thought she looked like a military fairy with her combat boots and purple bomber jacket.

"Nothing wrong with being a little neat," said Peter looking as though someone had taken away his favorite toy. "It makes finding things easier when you're organized."

Jenny pressed her ear against the door and wrinkled her face. "I can hear voices and some sort of tapping. Maybe they're rehearsing some tap-dancing moves for the next big Horizon dance-out challenge. I can totally picture the oracles line dancing with those giant crystals."

Peter pulled Jenny gently from the door. "Oracles don't dance, purple-head. They see into the future."

Jenny blew him a kiss and twirled away laughing.

"Shall we?" said David. And before anyone could answer, he kicked the door. It swung open easily. David marched across the threshold, followed quickly by Kara, Jenny and Peter. With a boom, the door shut behind them.

The gigantic circular room looked to be the size of half a level in Horizon—a world in itself. A cluster of sliding contraptions lined the perimeter of the room like a moving train. Golden smoke puffed out of the chimneys of this steam-powered assembly line. White fluff covered the floor like a foot of snow. At first Kara thought it was snowing, but quickly realized that the white flakes raining on them were from the hundreds of oracles chiseling away at huge boulders of transparent rock overhead. They stood on their crystal balls above a moving platform and sculpted their masterpieces feverishly.

Kara watched in awe as an oracle transformed one of the giant pieces of rock into a perfect crystal ball in a matter of seconds. The crystal shimmered and a light emanated from inside it. The oracle clapped excitedly and flung his tiny arms around his newborn crystal, sobbing in happiness.

She had never seen so many oracles in one place at the same time. The tiny men were hard at work, and Kara felt as if she had just stepped into Santa's workshop. She smiled. It was all strangely beautiful.

The sound of hammering and the constant puttering of the machine engines thundered around them like a great storm. Apart from the oracles working on the boulders, other oracles swept up mountains of the white fluff onto a second level where it was stored out of sight. Deep paths snaked around the chamber floor in intricate designs where the oracles had ploughed trails for the pedestrians. A few oracles stopped hammering and waved happily at the group.

"Come on, let's find who's in charge here." David lead the way on one of the trails, he was the only one who didn't seem impressed with their surroundings. Kara knew he was worried and angry. He hadn't said much since they left CDD.

Kara rushed to catch up to David, and Peter pulled Jenny along as she waved at the oracles. The sound of their heavy boots was muffled by the soft white particles from the crystals. After a few minutes of walking, they stood before a large in-ground pool. Steam rose from the silver-colored water that sparkled in the soft light. Twelve crystal spheres were half submerged in the water like eggs in a pot. One single crystal rested in the middle. Directly above it was an enormous spinning model of the solar system, with planets orbiting around the sun.

David whistled loudly. "Anyone care for a skinny-dip?"

It was the first time he had smiled since Ariel had told them all Kara would have to go on her next mission as a mortal. Kara needed him to smile, to show his usual confidence. His scowl hadn't reassured her. She needed David's encouragement and strength—if he didn't believe she could do it, then how could she believe she could?

Kara forced a smile. "Not sure the oracles would be happy to see your *uncovered* self."

"You never know, they might enjoy the show." David's expression darkened and hardened again.

Kara's knees buckled, and she felt her last thread of confidence drain away. She reached out and grabbed David's hand. "David, don't be angry. I need you to believe in me—"

"Uh...guys," said Peter, his eyes were wide, and he cocked his head forward.

Instinctively, Kara let go of David's hand as an oracle sped towards them.

"Hello, hello! Welcome, welcome!" The oracle's silver robes billowed behind him like a large rippling flag. He reminded Kara of a circus clown she had once seen performing a balancing act on a great rubber ball. White fluff rose and sprayed out on either side of his great crystal ball, like giant waves from a soaring boat. He came to a stop in front of them.

The oracle clapped his hands excitedly. "Welcome guardians! This is a very exhilarating occasion. We are going to perform the very *first* memory projection." He jumped with his finger in the air, slipped and steadied himself before he fell. "I do hope we get it right, it'll be our very first attempt with a non-oric."

"A what?" said Kara, smiling in spite of herself.

The oracle gave her a curious look. "A non-oric, of course— non-seers, non-clairvoyants—those without the inner eye. We've never done it before with a non-oric, so we'll just have to *see* what happens, won't we."

"Great, that's comforting," grumbled David. He crossed his arms over his chest and if Kara didn't know any better, she's have thought he was about to punch the oracle.

The oracle's piercing blue eyes searched the group and settled on Kara. His eyes widened. "And you must be the lucky winner! You are Kara, are you not?—the one with the tainted essence—the guardian chosen for the very *special,* never-heard-of assignment. A one-of-a-kind mission for a one-of-a-kind guardian."

The oracle's eyes shimmered, and Kara felt he might have been searching her body for her tainted part. She was being dissected like a lab rat, and she hated it. She fidgeted on the spot uncomfortably.

"Yup, that's me. I'm the lucky one."

She didn't feel lucky at all, in fact she felt as though she had been cursed. She looked over to Jenny, who gave her a worried smile. She felt the first stages of panic rise in her chest. Straining to remain calm, she looked over to the oracle.

"Oracle, so what's this memory projection? I don't remember ever hearing about it before," she said, glad her voice sounded even.

The oracle took a moment before answering. "Memory projection is what we oracles use to see the future, or the future of the world. It is a powerful tool, yet not an exact science, mind you."

The oracle scratched his head, lost in thought for a moment. Wisps of his long white hair wavered on the top of his head like tall grasses. "It's not always a hundred per cent accurate, you see. Futures change. They evolve and disappear only to be replaced by new ones. With every decision one makes, the path of one's future changes. Sometimes the future we see does not come to pass. In certain cases we can also use memory projection to change the course of the future, to alter one's path. But meddling with the future has its risks. Altering the future can be devastating...but let's not get into that right now."

The oracle tilted his head and lost his smile.

Kara was even more confused. It was no wonder the oracles were always a little bit off. She rubbed her temples feeling a jumbo headache on its way. "So how is this supposed to work on me? I'm not even sure why I'm here. How is this memory-projecting thing supposed to help me on my new assignment? Do I have to see into my future or something?"

The oracle stared into space. "Hmm? I'm sorry dear, what were we talking about?"

Kara frowned. "The memory projection? Remember?"

The oracle shook out of his trance, his smile returned. "Well of course dear! This is so exiting!" As he leaned forward slightly, his crystal ball squished the top of Kara's toes, and she just had enough time to pull them out before they got stuck. "You have been chosen to perform your next mission as a *mortal*."

"We already know that," interrupted David, "why don't you tell us something we don't already know."

The oracle's eyes had a cheery glow in them—the look of a mad scientist eager to demonstrate his latest invention. "You see, once you return to your mortal body," continued the oracle, "all your memories and abilities as a guardian will be lost to you. You will have no recollection of your guardian angel days. You will not remember your friends here, or me, for that matter. It will be just like before when you returned to Earth after your previous assignments. Your memory will be erased—"

The oracle snapped his fingers.

"...which is why we have decided to use the memory projection on you. It will help you remember and see through the *veil* of the supernatural. You'll be able to see your friends as guardian angels, and your eyes will be open to your enemies."

Kara could already see fragments of the supernatural as a mortal, but she kept that to herself for now. She didn't want to confuse the oracle. "So...once I'm back in my mortal body, I'm going to remember my mission as a guardian angel. Okay, I get it. Will it be instantaneous?"

"We hope so," said the oracle, not looking too convincing. His fingers twitched nervously at his side.

"Is it dangerous?" demanded David. "You said you've never done this before to a non-oric. So, you're not even sure it will work, am I right?"

The oracle folded his hands together. "We are *fairly* certain it will work on Miss Clara—".

"Fairly certain is *not* certain." David's voice rose, and he stepped forward towards the oracle.

"So there's a chance it won't work. What if something goes wrong, did you think of that? What if something bad happens to her? What if this hurts her, or she loses her mind? Have you thought of that?"

"It's all right, David," said Kara. "I'm sure it'll be fine," she lied and clasped her trembling hands behind her. "I've agreed to do this. It's my job. I have to stop the dark warlock from taking more souls. I need to save my mother. If I have to be mortal to do it, then so be it. It's a chance I have to take." She realized she sounded braver than she felt. She hoped that David was buying her performance.

"This is crazy!" David's voice trembled with rage. "She can't do this as a mortal! She won't be strong enough. Mortals are just a bag of blood and bones. She'll be vulnerable to demons, to the Seirs. She won't be able to defend herself. She'll be tortured and killed. I won't let you do this to her!"

"But you must," said the oracle in a soothing voice.

"I won't!"

"But you will." He fixed his eyes on David. "Clara must complete her mission as a *mortal* guardian. It is the only way to get close enough to the dark witch. As a guardian angel, you know the importance of the mortals and their souls. It will be your job to protect her once she joins her mortal body. She will rely on you and this group to protect her. We do not know if her elemental abilities will surface. But it is a chance we must take—for the sake of all the mortal souls in the world."

Kara didn't like the sound of that. As a guardian angel, she could always rely on her special elemental power, even though it was unpredictable. At least it was there as a safety net. Now she was going back out there to fight a demon with nothing. She felt naked, as defenseless as a mortal.

The ground shook suddenly, and Kara turned to see eleven more oracles approaching on their crystal balls. Their big smiles should have reassured her, but they didn't. She tried to smile back.

"Ah, here we are," the oracle smiled brightly as he greeted his brethren. "Now we may begin." The eleven oracles rolled their crystal balls around the pool in a straight line. One by one the oracles settled themselves in front of the pool and jumped off their crystal balls to land on the other crystals that were submerged into the water.

"It is time, Tara." The oracle stretched out his grubby little hand towards Kara. "Come now, we shall begin the memory projection." He joined the other oracles in the pool.

Kara's skin tingled. It was too late to back out now. She caught Jenny staring at her and offered her a brave smile, even though the worry in her eyes gave her away. David's cold gaze was fixed on the pool, and Peter tried unsuccessfully to blend into the background.

As she took a step forward, David grabbed her arm and steered her towards him.

"Wait, I have something for you." He pulled up the sleeve from his jacket and untied a thin brown leather bracelet. "Give me your wrist."

Obediently, Kara held out her left arm and watched David as he tied it securely around her wrist. Just by the way he was handling it, she knew it was important to him. She had seen the bracelet on David's wrist many times, but had never thought of asking where he'd gotten it or why he wore it. It had never seemed important at the time. It looked like a regular leather bracelet with strips of leather braided together with a few multicolored beads. Was this David's way of saying their relationship was going to the next level?

"Why are you giving me this?" she asked awkwardly. Her mouth felt like it was full of cotton balls. He had never given her anything before, and it made her even more nervous.

"It's my lucky charm," said David. "I've had it since my first assignment as a guardian. I was overconfident and stupid, and I failed to save the mortal. He was a guy around my age...he even kinda looked like me in a weird way. Anyway, I managed to save his soul, but it wasn't good enough, I should have saved him, too. He had this bracelet on him, so I took it to remember him...I never wanted to forget." He stared at the ground for a moment. "It's always brought me luck, and I think you should have it now."

Kara felt like her chest was going to burst. She didn't know what to say. She wanted to kiss him, but everyone was waiting for her and watching.

"David...I can't accept this..."

"Didn't your mother tell you it's impolite to refuse a gift?" He teased. "You need this more than me, and I'll feel better knowing that you have it."

She rolled the bracelet gently over her wrist. "Thanks David, this means a lot."

"Miss Tara!" called the oracle. "We need to start the projection. Hurry up please!"

Kara and David locked eyes for a moment before she pulled herself away reluctantly. With her fingers still twisting the bracelet, she made her way to the edge of the pool and watched her silver reflection waver in the water, like a foggy memory of the girl she once was.

With some effort, the oracle leaped above the water and landed effortlessly on a crystal ball. "Right then," he said. "You must stand on the middle crystal, Tara. Once you're settled, then we shall begin."

Kara was just about to tell him her name was Kara and not Tara, but she bit her tongue. She looked around. She felt like she was part of some weird ritual where the girl would be placed in the middle of a circle and then cut into tiny pieces as offerings to some pagan god. All of a sudden, the pool seemed very cold and uninviting.

Someone grabbed her hand and pulled her around. Jenny smothered Kara in a bear hug and whispered in her ear. "See you on the other side, girl."

Kara smiled uncertainly and let go of Jenny gently, like she was forced to do so, even thought she didn't want to.

"Good luck, Kara," said Peter awkwardly. "I'm sure everything will be all right. We'll see you soon."

Kara smiled and tried to answer, but the words died in her throat.

David edged closer and interlaced his fingers with hers. His face was so close that she was tempted to kiss him. She forced the thought out of her head.

"If it doesn't feel right, you jump off." His blue eyes pierced into hers. "If it hurts, or you know something is wrong, you get off. You get me?"

Kara found her voice. "I will, don't worry. I'm sure the oracles know what they're doing...hopefully. "

But Kara was terrified. It took her some time to let go of David's fingers.

She stood by the edge of the pool. The water looked like melted iron. Her feet felt like concrete blocks.

She lifted her right boot and stepped into the pool.

The silver water only rose to her knees, and she relaxed a little. She swished her fingers through the water. It was thicker than normal water, like liquid soap. It was cool, but not uncomfortably cool. She climbed easily on the top of the crystal in the middle of the circle and stood up, waiting.

She looked to David who gave her a thumbs up and a quivering smile.

"One more thing," said the oracle, "If you die as a mortal, then the link will be lost. And we will not be able to perform another memory projection on you. It can only be done once. If we do it again, your soul will be destroyed. A mortal soul cannot take that much projection." All the oracles bobbed their heads up and down in agreement.

"So if I die as a mortal, then I won't be able to finish the job," said Kara. "The dark warlock will win. I get it."

"Sometimes sacrifices are inevitable," said the oracle. "The blood of the one that walks alone will free the souls."

Kara wasn't sure what that meant. She hated when oracles spoke in riddles, and she didn't feel like trying to understand it at that moment, since she was already scared to death.

"Let us begin." All the oracles lifted their arms in the air. Kara watched anxiously and wondered if she should lift her arms, too. She grabbed hold of the bracelet and twisted it with her fingers, grateful for its small comfort.

Crack!

Electricity filled the air above the pool. Kara's clothes and hair flapped in an invisible wind. A coolness sucked out the hot air. The oracles reached out and clasped their hands together in a circle around her.

Kara watched mesmerized. Their blue eyes glazed over with a golden color. They started to chant in a language that Kara couldn't recognize. As their chanting grew louder, thunder rumbled overhead. Jenny and Peter stepped backwards with fear in their eyes. But David stood still. His fingers were curled into fists and his eyes locked onto Kara with an expression as if to say, '*say the word and I'll come get you*'. Part of her wanted him to.

Lightning flashed from crystal to crystal, until they were all connected like a white-hot spider web. Kara's feet slid, and she strained to keep her balance. The silver waters bubbled and mist coiled above its surface. She didn't want to slip and fall in.

Suddenly the water from the pool rose all around and formed a ring around Kara and the oracles. David and the others disappeared behind the wall of rolling water. She was inside a tornado of water. The chanting grew even louder. She thought she heard David calling out to her, but there was too much noise to hear anything clearly.

A bright light burned her eyes. It was miracle she still stood on the crystal ball. She blinked the blotches away. Images appeared on the water like a giant movie projection. Kara watched amazed as images of people, places and things blurred passed her as though they were on fast forward. The images began to slow until she could make sense of them. She saw faces of different men and women and children. She saw a field of orange poppies swaying in the wind, then a city's skylight.

Then the images shifted, and she saw her reflection in the water.

She saw herself walking down the street with her portfolio and cell phone. A scream died in her throat as she witnessed her body slam against the front of a bus. The images changed. She saw herself standing in the elevator with Chimp 5M51. Then she was a guardian, fighting shadow demons with David. The image shifted again, and she saw herself at a breakfast table, laughing with her mom. A blur, then she was in the Netherworld fighting a higher demon with David. More and more images of her life as a mortal and as a guardian flashed before her eyes. She felt dizzy. She wavered on the spot. Her body felt cold. The visions spun faster and faster. Her head throbbed, and she screamed. Her mind was on fire. A bolt of energy flashed through her like chill. She looked down. Her body was enflamed in white fire.

The white fire exploded. Kara screamed, and her body disappeared.

CHAPTER 4

AMNESIA

KARA KNEW SHE WAS DYING.

She closed her eyes and let it come. It was only a matter of time now before her heart stopped pumping oxygen to her brain. She had no idea one person could lose so much blood. She sat in a pool of her own blood, and she could smell it. The demon had killed her.

She was numb. She could feel herself drifting towards sleep. It was too late to get to a hospital. She would never have the chance to tell David how she truly felt. She would die cold and wet in a dark alley with a stranger who held her hand and knew her name...

But death wouldn't come.

Then a gush of warmth spread through her as though she had been submerged in a hot bath. The veil of weakness lifted and was replaced by a surge of strength. She trembled as blood gushed to her limbs. She sucked cool air into her lungs and felt warm again. Her heart pounded strongly in her chest. She opened her eyes.

It was dark, and snowflakes gleamed under the streetlight that flickered and buzzed. She blinked her snow-crusted eyelashes. A full moon peeked through thick navy-blue clouds.

A young man peered down at her.

Kara sat upright.

The stranger smiled warmly. Snow fell from his tousled blond head. His clothes were covered in snow. As he searched her face, Kara looked away, abashed. There was something about his piercing blue eyes that unsettled her. It was as if they could see her deepest thoughts and secrets.

She strained to see into the darkness, suddenly anxious. Where was the creature that had attacked her? She remembered a flash of red light. The creature had attacked her. She remembered the piercing pain. She was bleeding. Instinctively her hand went to her leg. She wriggled her fingers through the rip in her jeans and pressed her hand on her skin. There was no gaping wound. She searched the ground around her. Not a drop of blood anywhere. What was going on? Had she imagined the whole thing? Impossible...

"Kara, how are you feeling?" said the stranger in a voice that made Kara's skin ripple with goose bumps. Where had she heard that voice before?

She stared at the stranger, frowning. "How do you know my name?"

There was something very familiar with this guy, but she couldn't figure it out. Who was he?

The stranger leaned forward with an anxious look on his face. For a moment he just stood there, rocking back and forth on his heels, staring at her uncertainly. "It's me...David...don't you recognize me?"

"Nope. I only know one David, and you're not him."

Kara pushed herself back onto her feet, surprised at her own strength. She felt better with her feet on the ground. Apart from the rip in her jeans, there was no sign that anything had attacked her. She couldn't help but wonder if she had imagined the whole thing and that she was going mad.

The stranger's face fell, and Kara felt a sting in her chest. He backed away slowly, his eyes never leaving hers. He raked his fingers through his hair. "Maybe it needs time to work."

Kara brushed her hands on her jeans. "What does? And how do you know me again? Do we share a class together or something—you kinda look familiar to me."

Her fingers were stiff and cold. "Do you see any mitts on the ground?"

"What's the last thing you remember?" said the stranger as he studied her face.

"Why? What's it to you?" Kara kicked the snow with her boots looking for her mitts.

"It's important."

Giving up on her mitts, Kara jammed her hands in her coat pockets and searched the street. "Well, I was on my way to the drugstore when something attacked me. It's a bit blurry. I think I hit my head and passed out."

She wasn't about to tell a complete stranger that a demon had tried to kill her and by some miracle she had survived. He would definitely think she was as mad as a hatter.

The stranger watched her closely. "You don't remember anything else...anything at all?"

"Like I told you, *no*."

He pointed at her left arm. "So—who gave you that bracelet then?"

"I'm not wearing a brace—" the rest of the word died in her throat. A leather bracelet was wrapped around her left wrist. Kara narrowed her eyes. How did that get there? She didn't remember putting it on. But one thing was for certain—it wasn't hers. So, who's was it?

The stranger eyed her worriedly. "I gave you that bracelet. Don't you remember?"

Kara didn't like the intense way the stranger was looking at her. He looked a little crazy, and she didn't have time to fight off crazies right now.

"Look, *David*, if that's your real name, I don't know you, sorry. Listen, thanks for watching out for me...but I need to get going. My mother needs me."

The stranger stepped up to Kara. "What do you *see* when you look at me?"

Kara raised her brows and tried hard not to laugh. "I see a guy in a flimsy leather jacket who's probably freezing. It's December you know, *winter*—you probably need to put on a warmer jacket."

His jaw clenched, and he started to pace around nervously. Where had she seen him before? He was acting a lot like someone she knew...but who? She just couldn't figure it out.

"You don't see anything different about me...about my skin?" His voice rose slightly in alarm.

Kara shook her head and wiped the snow from her eyes. "Nope, sorry. Should I? It looks pretty normal beige to me. I don't see what you mean by *different*."

She was beginning to think this guy was a little off. She should be wary of strangers, but somehow she felt comfortable around him. It was like being around an old friend, even though he wasn't. She pulled her hood over her head and shifted her weight uncomfortably. Something was off about him all right...but what?

Kara exhaled, her breath coiled around her in a white mist. But the stranger's mouth was mist-less. He didn't appear to be breathing at all. Kara waited and watched for vapors to come out of his nose. Nothing. A tinge of fear rippled inside her. If he wasn't breathing, that meant he wasn't human. If he wasn't human...then what was he?

The guy pulled up his sleeve and waved his bare arm in front of Kara. "You don't see it glowing? You don't see through the veil?"

"Glowing? Veil?" Kara laughed nervously and stepped back. She didn't want to offend him, but he was acting a little schizo, and he still wasn't breathing. "Are you feeling all right?" she said, "Are you sure *you* didn't bump your head—"

The rest of Kara's words caught in her throat. Suddenly, the stranger's forearm started to glow faintly as though liquid light flowed through his veins. She looked up. Where his skin had been a normal beige color moments before, it now radiated a soft yellow light. She could see two stars etched across his forehead, as though he had been branded.

"What are you? You're not human!" Kara backed away from him again, frightened. What if he was a demon disguised as a hot guy, just to trick her? The stranger had appeared at the exact moment that the creature that had attacked her had disappeared. What if they were working together?

The stranger lifted his hands up. "Kara, don't be afraid, I won't hurt you. It's me, *David*. Don't you recognize me? You know me, remember? We've fought in the legion together. We've combated demons, saved mortal souls, we're friends—well, maybe more than friends."

"I don't know you," said Kara. But somehow it felt like a lie. She let out a sigh of frustration. "What is going on? Why do I feel like I know you and then don't? And please tell me why you're glowing?"

"Because I'm in my M-suit—my mortal suit. I'm an angel, Kara," said the stranger in a soothing voice. He drew closer and reached out to grab her hand.

ZAP!

Kara jumped back. An electric shock surged through her from his touch. It was like touching an electrical outlet with her fingers.

"What was that?"

The stranger shook his head bewildered. He stared at his hands. "I don't know. It's never happened before. Maybe because you're mortal, and I'm in my M-suit."

Kara took another step back. She couldn't find her voice. She breathed heavily and stared at the stranger through her icicle-clustered eyelashes that kept sticking together every time she blinked. In a weird way, she believed him. But how could she? She was definitely losing her mind. Angels? Could he really be an angel? He was freaking glowing!

"You can see through the veil now, the cloak that hides us from regular mortal eyes," said the stranger, as relief spread quickly to his face. "That's how you can see my skin glowing a little; it's my angel essence beneath this mortal suit. It's how you were able to see the demon that attacked you. You can see angels and demons, Kara."

That part she knew was true. Lately she had been seeing more and more ghastly creatures in the night. She always felt them near her, their evil sneaking up on her. But angels?

Kara watched the snow nestle gently on his head. "So, how come I can see these demons, like you say?" She thought about telling him that her mom could see them, too, but decided against it. He was a stranger after all. She didn't want to tell him her whole life's story.

"Because you're part elemental."

"I'm what?" Kara nearly choked. Wild-eyed, she stared at him. *Elemental*, she repeated. Somehow that word did sound familiar.

The stranger David kicked the ground in frustration. Puffs of snow flew in the air. "I knew it wouldn't work!" he yelled. "I knew it! I told them, but *nooooo*, they didn't believe me. Idiots!"

Kara pressed her hands on her head. "What didn't work? You're not making any sense. What's an elemental? If you know so much, then how come I can see these demons? And why are they attacking me? Tell me—"

"Soon." He grabbed her sleeve, careful not to touch her skin and steered her towards him.

"I need to get you to the safe house. Come on. Let's get you out of the cold." He pulled her into a jog, but Kara wrestled out of his grip.

"Let go of me! You know something about me, don't you? Why can I see these things and you...I've seen you before, haven't I? I can see it in your face. You're hiding something. I'm not going anywhere with you unless you tell me what's going on."

Kara crossed her arms over her chest and stood her ground.

"It's complicated," said the stranger a little annoyed. "Very complicated..."

"I like complicated." Kara raised her brows. "Go ahead. I'm waiting."

He let out an exasperated sigh. "You won't even believe me if I tell you. It's pointless, and we're wasting time. We should go before it gets dangerous—"

"Try me."

"Fine," said the stranger. "You're a guardian angel, just like me. You can see demons and angels, just like me. And right now you're on a special assignment as a mortal. There—you happy now? Good, we have to go—"

"This is crazy," said Kara, even though she felt everything he said was true. "I'm not going anywhere with you. I don't know you."

The stranger grabbed her by the shoulders and made her face him. "*I'm* David. It's me. There is no other David. I know this isn't making any sense right now, but believe me; *I'm* your guy. Trust me on this, Kara. *I'm* David!"

Kara stared into the stranger's blue eyes. They were a lot like David's, which was weird. He had the same nose, same square jaw, same hair, same little scar on his chin, same little dimples when he smiled, he even smelled like David, but at the same time he appeared different. He wore the brown leather jacket, black T-shirt and faded jeans that looked a lot like David's. In fact, they were identical in every way, down to the maroon stain on the jacket's left shoulder.

Her jaw fell open. "Where did you get these clothes?"

He turned his head quickly, as though he heard something. Then he pulled a silver dagger from his jacket and stood protectively in front of Kara. Somehow, she wasn't surprised to see the weapon in his hand. She looked over his shoulder and followed his gaze.

A shadow clambered down the street towards them. It was huge, with glowing red eyes and gangly limbs. It moved like a wild animal, but somehow its movements were jagged and twisted. At first, Kara thought it was a regular dog, but it was too big to be a dog. It moved into the light. Instead of fur, tentacles covered its back like coiling snakes. It focused its glowing red on Kara. Black pus oozed from its body and dripped onto the snow like hot oil. A gust of cool wind brought with it the smell of rotten flesh. Its unnatural growl cut through the eerie silence. A chill rolled up her spine. Kara winced at the sound of its nails scraping the pavement, like knives down a blackboard. Her heart pounded in her ears. Then a second identical creature joined it, then another. As soon as she saw them, she knew they were evil.

"Hound demons," said the stranger through gritted teeth.

Kara took a step back. "They don't look very friendly—"

He grabbed her hand, and Kara felt a jolt of electricity surge from his fingers.

"They're not. RUN!"

CHAPTER 5

BRAIN-ZAPPING

KARA DID NOT WANT to be demon dog kibble. She liked the stranger's grip on her hand as they raced down the street, even if it did feel a little *electrifying*. He was fast, really fast, with super strength. He had to be an angel. There was no other explanation, unless he was Superman's half-brother. He pulled her along like a doll, as though she didn't weigh anything at all. Her feet soared above the pavement and only touched solid ground every few seconds. It was the closest thing to flying she'd ever experienced. She stole a look behind her.

The hound demons ran like giant grey wolves on steroids. She wasn't sure the stranger's super speed would be fast enough. They made her skin crawl. And soon they would catch up to them.

"Behind—us—the—demons," said Kara trying to catch her breath. "Go—faster!"

Suddenly, the stranger spun Kara around, and in the same movement he propelled his body forward and threw his dagger with his other arm. It sliced through the air like a bullet and perforated the closest creature's head with a *thud*. The beast stumbled and toppled over with an ear splitting howl. Kara covered her ears with her hands as the demon hound convulsed and twitched, its skin sizzling and popping like oil in a frying pan. Within seconds there was nothing left but a small pile of black ashes in the white snow.

Kara searched the darkness for the other creatures. Something moved up the street between two buildings. But when she blinked, whatever it was had disappeared.

"Where did the other two go? They were right there?" she said.

"I don't know, but they're not far. Probably watching us right now, waiting for us to make a mistake."

Kara inspected the remains. "Is it dead? It looks pretty dead to me."

"For now. Its spirit is back in the Netherworld where it belongs," answered the stranger.

He swept the ground near the kill, picked up his silver dagger, wiped it clean on his jeans, and sheathed it back inside his jacket. "We can't stay out here it's too dangerous. I have to get you to the safe house where the demons won't be able to sense us."

Kara brushed the ashes with her boot. "What are these things anyway? One minute they were solid, and the next they just disintegrated into dust, like some weird spontaneous combustion phenomenon."

"Hound demons are hunters and guardians of the Netherworld. They're expert trackers and killers. Think of them like police dogs, only bigger and a million times more evil—and they're here to kill *you*. Someone sent them after us."

The stranger grabbed her hand jolting her with electricity again.

"They found our scent, and once they're locked on to it—there's nothing to be done. They'll hunt us down forever if they have to. They'll never stop until they destroy you, and more will come. We have to get out of here—it's not safe for you anymore."

As if on cue, an angry pack of giant rabid hound demons crawled from the shadows and advanced slowly towards them. The growling hounds lifted their noses in the air, smelling their scent. Kara felt like a hundred ants were crawling up her spine. Her heart pounded in her ears.

"I'll never be rid of them, right? They'll always find me no matter where I go?" She knew it was true.

"You're like a demon-magnet," said the strange David, glancing quickly at her. "You've always been. But this is weird—I've never seen so many at once. Usually they're sent as a *pair*—not a *pack*. I can't fight them all. We'll have to make a run for it."

The hounds howled and charged.

"Unless you want to become a new brand of dog food, we have to go!"

He pulled Kara and ran until her legs were on fire and felt like concrete blocks. Every breath was like swallowing razor blades. Her throat was raw. She couldn't keep going. The guy who called himself David didn't even break a sweat. Maybe angels didn't have the need to perspire? She hoped he would need water and rest. How far was the nice warm safe house?

The foul smell from the hound demons burned Kara's nostrils. She swallowed back the bile in her throat and tried to breathe through her mouth, but the cold air scorched her throat.

They sprinted down another dark street, turned a corner and tall street lamps illuminated the dark like brilliant stars, and Kara could see where they were going. The David guy didn't seem to mind the darkness. Did angels see in the dark? Kara shivered in a cold sweat. If she didn't get warm soon, she would get sick or die of exhaustion.

The wild wails and scraping nails of the beasts tearing down the street behind them were so close that Kara could almost feel their foul breath on the back of her neck. If they didn't get to safety soon, they were dog-chow.

A green street sign caked with snow read: Saint-Marc. The street was covered in drifting snow and the shops that lined either side were dark and closed.

All except for one. They raced towards the soft yellow light that emanated from a shop nestled between *Mario's all you can eat Pizzeria* and *One-eye Bill's Bakery*. As she staggered forward, Kara turned—her heart skipped.

The hound demons were feet away. Their putrid hot breath made her gag. She lost her footing and tripped. In an instant the stranger grabbed her jacket and pulled her up just as a giant claw slashed so near her face she could smell its stink of rotten flesh.

The stranger pushed Kara forward, to protect her with his body.

He turned to face the demons.

He hit the first one between the eyes with a powerful blow, and the beast fell to the side—only to be replaced by another larger one. Its sharp fangs snapped towards his face and the tentacles on its head lashed out at him like a nest of hungry snakes. He screamed and when he pulled the barbed tentacle from his neck, brilliant light seeped from the gash on his skin.

Kara was breathing hard. She heard a grunt and turned to see rows of pointy teeth that glimmered in the dark like the jaws of a great white shark. Red eyes glowered with hatred. Kara was staring at death. Instinctively, she kicked out with her leg and managed to make crunch her boots into its head.

The creature howled and leaped for her throat—

The front door of *Jim's Old Bookstore* exploded open.

Mr. Patterson charged madly into the street with two glowing crystal balls the size of grapefruits in his hands. He whipped them hard towards the demon hounds, one after another, like a baseball pitcher. The stranger pulled Kara down, and the crystals soared inches above their heads.

The ground shook. Thunder and lightning cackled overhead, and an intense white light illuminated the street.

The demon hounds' bodies blazed in white fire. The creatures tore at their own skin, howling. And then they dissolved and the fire subsided. Except for the piles of ashes on the white snow, the street was deserted. The hounds were destroyed.

Kara stood up on shaky legs—amazed she could still stand. She held the cramp at her side. Her throat burned with every intake of air, and she choked and coughed as she fought for air. She wiped her wet face with the sleeve of her jacket.

"Filthy creatures! How dare you show yourselves on my street! Go back to the Netherworld!" spat Mr. Patterson.

He paced around the street, kicking up snow as he went.

"And don't ever think of coming back, you hear? I'm warning you, keep your *dogs* on a leash! The light will always prevail! Darkness will never conquer the light!"

Kara had no idea who he was ranting at out there in his Hawaiian shirt and green Bermuda shorts.

Mr. Patterson turned and beamed at Kara and the stranger.

"Ah! Finally, there you are. You're a half hour late. I was beginning to worry. Messy business this is, sending hound demons in the streets—*my* street. Dark days are coming, mark my words—I have seen it. We mustn't linger, there are worse things than hound demons out tonight. Come inside, quickly."

He waddled past them hurriedly, mumbling to himself and then disappeared through the front door of his shop.

"Mr. Patterson?" Kara watched her boss disappear behind the door.

She tensed, a cold shiver on the back of her neck. The stranger was staring at her like she was some sort of experiment gone wrong.

"So...this is your safe house? Is this for real? I work here!"

"Come on," he said. "We'll explain everything to you inside."

Before she could argue that she wasn't going in until he explained himself, the guy turned and pushed open the front door. Curiosity and the fear of more hound demons got the best of her.

As she stepped across the doormat she could hear muffled voices. Wind chimes sang faintly from above the front door as she pushed in.

Jim's Old Bookstore was in its usual borderline—hoarding state. The air smelled like a mixture of old glue and mildew, and the single flickering light bulb on the loose wire in the center of the shop illuminated the dust particles like miniature snowflakes. Crooked stacks of books teetered perilously in piles that went all the way up to the ceiling.

Mr. Patterson stood behind a glass case on the right side of the shop, frantically polishing a crystal ball as if it were stained, and he couldn't get it out no matter how much he buffed it.

Movement in the back of the store caught Kara's eye. A girl around her age emerged from behind a bookshelf. She looked like a combat elf, with sharp features and a short purple pixie-like haircut. She wore a purple bomber-style jacket, black cargo pants and matching purple boots.

A shy, nerdy-looking boy with glasses followed closely behind her. He fidgeted nervously and eyed everything in the shop with great interest. He was dressed in the same military-style black clothes, and finished the look with a green T-shirt that read, *Nerds rule!* Their skin gave off a subtle glow, just like the stranger's.

The girl came skipping towards Kara. "So—how does it feel? Are you filled with *disgustingly* sappy mortal emotions? Are you all giddy inside? Do you feel like crying all the time? God, I miss a good cry. Is it different from when you're in an M-suit? I bet it is."

The girl smiled, her large green eyes sparkled like giant emeralds.

Kara stepped away from the girl.

"You're an angel, too—aren't you? And him," she said, pointing a shaking finger at the boy.

It was warm inside but somehow she was still shaking. She wrapped her arms around herself. Why were there angels in Mr. Patterson's bookstore?

She watched as the girl and the stranger who called himself David exchanged a worried look.

"She doesn't remember anything," he told them. "It didn't work."

His face was deflated, and he kept glancing at Kara as though she might fall to pieces at any moment. She felt as if she had just walked in on a private conversation, everyone knew what the subject in question was—except her. It annoyed her a little.

"But they told us it would work on her?" said the boy with the glasses. "This doesn't make sense—oracles don't usually get anything wrong?"

The girl examined Kara closer.

"Nothing, really? You don't know who I am?" she asked Kara, and then she lowered her voice, as if somehow that would help her remember. "It's me...Jenny, your gal pal. I was the first GA to greet you on your very first day at CDD. Don't you remember?"

Kara shook her head.

"Never—seen—you—before—in—my—life," she said.

Kara was cold—her teeth chattered together. Her nose began to run, and she wished she had a Kleenex.

"Oh dear," said Mr. Patterson.

He placed his crystal gently beneath his glass counter and made his way towards them. His bare feet slapped the wood floors, and his large footprints smeared the top layer of grime. "Now we're in a pickle."

"You think? You oracles told us that it would work. Obviously, it didn't." The strange David guy paced around the room in a rage and punched the nearest bookshelf. It wavered and a selection of books banged to the floor.

Mr. Patterson ignored the guy's tantrum and clasped Kara's hands into his. His eyebrows shot up. "Dear me, your hands are cold as ice!"

"I lost my mitts," said Kara grumpily. "My mom knitted them for me." Her throat throbbed and her eyes began to burn.

She hated herself for forgetting about her mom. Her mother still needed medication—she had to get out of here. She forced herself not to think of her mother. She didn't want to cry in front of these strangers.

Mr. Patterson smiled kindly. "Well, let me fetch you a cup of hot chocolate to warm you up. And if I'm not mistaken, I think you've left a pair of mittens here. Just a second dear."

"I'd like that, thank you," said Kara.

Mr. Patterson disappeared behind his counter, clicked on a microwave, and returned moments later with a cup of hot chocolate and a pair of grey and black wool mitts.

Kara wrapped her stiff fingers around the warm cup. She took a sip. The hot chocolate warmed her and soothed her throat. It rejuvenated her.

"So that memory-charm thing didn't work, then, huh," said Jenny looking worried. "That's a real bummer. They said they could only do it once—so what are we going to do? Ariel told us that Kara was the only one going on the job as a mortal. It's not like *we* could do it?"

"It's much worse than that," said the stranger David angrily. "Somehow, she's attracting more demons than before. That pack of hound demons nearly finished us. Whatever the oracles did to her, they marked her as an easy target. It's like she has a sign on her forehead that reads, *free soul for demons—come and get it.*" He turned to Mr. Patterson and his expression darkened.

Mr. Patterson frowned. His eyes disappeared into his wrinkles. "Oh, dear, I'm afraid we had not thought about that. If you're right, then she's tainted—in more than one way. Her *true* self is exposed."

"Exposed?" Kara watched the scene unfold like a miniseries on television except that it was about her!

"Like a guardian without an M-suit," said Mr. Patterson matter of factly.

Jenny's jaw dropped. "A skinned chicken. Now that sucks."

The stranger David pulled at his hair. "I should have never let her do this! I should have known it wouldn't have worked! The legion has always used her to their advantage. And now she's as good as—"

"As what?" said Kara, "...dead?"

She stared at the guy, challenging him to speak his mind. He opened his mouth, but no words came out, then he looked away. Something about his nervous expression made her uncomfortable. Could there be some truth to what he was saying?

"Oh, man," the nerdy guy with the glasses rubbed his forehead. "How is she supposed to complete her mission like this? She doesn't even know who we are. We should head back to CDD and brief Ariel. I mean—we're stuck aren't we? It's not like we can move forward with the mission now, with her like that."

"This royally sucks." Jenny threw herself in a chair and crossed her arms over her chest.

"Mr. Patterson," said Kara as she edged into the group. "What's going on? Do you know these people?"

She wanted to say angels, but she felt it would just be too weird asking him that.

Mr. Patterson sighed. "Yes, dear, I do. And so do you, but you just don't remember."

"But I don't." Kara shook her head and did her best to hide her annoyance. "I've never seen them before. I think I would remember them—they glow in the dark."

"See? What do we do now?" shouted the stranger David, before Kara could ask another question. "We're finished! There's no way we can get to the witch now. Let's face it, the mission's over. We're done."

Kara frowned as she repeated the word *witch* in her mind. What was that about?

"It is not as bad as it seems. We foresaw a few *flaws* in the procedure," Mr. Patterson twirled his white beard between his fingers. He was silent for a moment then said, "I believe she just needs a little *push*—in order for her memories to return. But we must move quickly before the projection wears off completely."

The stranger David stopped dead in his tracks. "What kind of push? You better not mess this up more. I'm afraid I might go a little crazy in your store."

With a hop in his step, Mr. Patterson scurried over behind his counter. He pulled the sliding top across and grabbed the largest of his crystal balls. As he held it up, it glistened in the light like a miniature moon. He grinned like a schoolboy.

"We need to jump-start her brain."

Kara's mouth fell open. "You want to do what to my brain?"

Mr. Patterson suddenly looked a lot like a miniature Dr. Frankenstein—he had a crazed mad-scientist look in his eye.

"I don't think I want you to do anything to my brain," she continued, "I like my brain the way it is, thank you."

The tiny old man hurried over, cradling his crystal ball like a newborn child. "It won't hurt, dear, I promise." His eyes widened. "Actually, it might sting just a little—"

"It'll bring back her memories," interrupted stranger David, "you're quite sure it'll work? Are you a hundred percent positive, old man?"

"We'll just have to see, won't we? But I believe that just the right amount of crystal propulsion should do the trick. Just a little *zap*! But we must hurry."

Mr. Patterson measured Kara. "I can hardly see the projection on her anymore. It's fading. Quickly now."

Kara frowned. "H—e—l—l—o—I'm right here! And I don't want anyone doing anything to my brain. Do you hear me?"

Mr. Patterson ignored Kara and looked over to Jenny. "Penny, can you bring your chair over here, please."

Jenny shook her head and shrugged. "Penny was our dog, Mr. P."

She jumped up and shoved her chair over to Kara. "Sit," she ordered with a huge smile. "You be a good girl now."

Kara stood her ground. "Just a second, none of this is making any sense—"

The stranger David reached out and held Kara's hand. She cringed at the electric shock that pulsed through her palm again. "Trust me, Kara. You *need* to do this. It'll all make sense soon, I promise. The Kara I know would want this. She would want to remember—she would want to finish the mission."

Kara pursed her lips. She was in a room packed with angels and Dr. Frankenstein, who was about to fry her brain. No big deal. To top it off, demons were trying to kill her, and her mother lay dying from an incurable virus. What could be worse? She couldn't shake off the feeling that the stranger David was telling the truth— somehow she trusted him.

Against her better judgment, she sank into the chair and shrugged. "Now what?"

"Hold this in your hands." Mr. Patterson handed the crystal ball to Kara.

"It might feel hot and you could get a shock, but whatever happens...don't drop it," he said. "It would be very bad if you did. Stand back everyone!" He let go of the sphere, lifted his arms dramatically, and jumped back.

Kara wanted to reply that she wasn't planning on dropping it, but as soon as her hands touched the crystal, her body stiffened, and a series of images flashed in her mind's eye. It was like a television had turned on inside her head.

She saw herself fighting misshapen demons with glowing red eyes. Then she jumped into a pool of salt water and watched as her body sparkled and dissolved into tiny particles. Next she was tied to a chair as a mechanical man drained her of her blood. The images changed again, and she saw herself fighting against a group of evil-looking bald men with eyes tattooed to the back of their heads. She wanted to scream. The images shifted—golden electricity danced along her body until she was ablaze in golden fire.

She clamped her hands tightly around the crystal as a wave of cool energy washed through her. Her legs shook. The crystal suddenly felt heavy in her hands. Her hands started to sweat, and she felt her fingers slip. She strained to hang on. Faster and faster the images flashed inside her mind, until she felt she might go mad...

Silence. The last images wavered and disappeared. Kara blinked. Sweat dripped down her back, and her heart raced like she had run a marathon. She rolled the crystal ball gently in her clammy hands.

She remembered. She remembered it all!

Kara looked up—she recognized his face. He had been telling the truth all along.

"David, I'm so sorry."

David beamed. "Welcome back."

CHAPTER 6

BOSCASTLE VILLAGE, CORNWALL

KARA HATED AIRPLANES.

It wasn't so much the actual plane, but rather the feeling of not being in control. What was worse was the constant throbbing pain in her head that had begun at Mr. Patterson's shop. The jump-start on her brain had worked all right, but she couldn't stop feeling that something had gone terribly wrong.

As the captain announced their descent, she grabbed her chair's armrests, her heart in her throat. They would be landing shortly—the death-ride would soon be over.

She could make out the outline of Cornwall through the white puffy clouds. Villages glittered in the sun along a long strip of land surrounded by a blue ocean. Boats and cottages lined the shore. Vast fields and mountains spread out into the distance, and tiny homes speckled the snow-covered land.

Kara and her team had not been separated for such a long period of time before. She had had to fly alone—she couldn't do any of the supernatural GA things to which she had been accustomed. She felt more alienated from the legion than ever.

She pulled at the leather bracelet that David had given her. For something so small, it somehow made her feel safe, and she took comfort from it.

Kara hadn't slept. While rest of the group would have used the pools to Vega themselves to Cornwall, she had endured eight hours of moldy cheese, BO and the screaming of children who kept kicking the back of her seat. The adrenaline from being chased by demons and then getting her memory jump-started was yet to subside. She couldn't stop replaying the events from the day before over and over in her head.

She thought of her mom, and her insides twisted. The only chance her mother and the others had of fighting the warlock's virus was if Kara could kill him. And she swore that she would—no matter what.

Kara wiped her sweaty palms on her jeans and tried to breathe normally. She needed a dark witch, who despised angels, to help her defeat a dark warlock—and she needed to fight him as a mortal. The only thing going for her was that she remembered how to use her blade.

The archangel Ariel had told her that every minute the dark warlock killed another hundred souls. They had about two and a half days before the winter solstice, so they would need to find the dark witch quickly. No pressure.

Kara was thrown gently forward as the airplane made contact with the runway. The seatbelt light went off and with her backpack secured comfortably on her shoulders she followed the horde out of the plane and made her way through the airport.

"Kara! Over here!"

Kara spotted David, Peter, and Jenny standing near the main exit. David looked hotter than ever. And to top it off, he was freaking glowing. With his blond hair and brilliant golden skin, he looked like a glowing god. It wasn't fair.

Jenny welcomed her with her usual bear hug and Peter just smiled awkwardly, looking for something to do with his hands. Much to Kara's horror, Ashley and her team came strolling towards them. She met Ashley's glare and didn't look away.

"What are *you* doing here?" said Kara, with a little more malice than she intended.

Ashley flipped her long blond braid off her shoulder and smiled. Her sharp features twisted in mock humor. "What? You're not pleased to see me?" She laughed and turned to her team who grunted in approval.

For the first time, Kara really looked at Ashley's team. They were all about the same age as her group, between sixteen or seventeen years old. Sasha was a mousy girl. She was short with shoulder length straw-like hair and blinked her eyes like she was trying to focus. She fidgeted nervously behind Ashley. Raymond was thick and tall, with red hair and a face like a bloodsucker. Ling had a thin face and long fingers that looked like they needed something to do. He had the long black greasy hair of some grunge band member. His black eyes never left Ashley. Kara was sure he sought her approval, like a good little puppy.

"We're here in case you fail, *freak*." Ashley sneered, and her minions snorted.

Heat rose to Kara's face. "Who said anything about failing? I've *never* failed an assignment, and I'm not about to start now."

But Kara didn't feel so sure of herself. The truth was she was utterly terrified going on this mission as a mortal. She felt her eyes sting and struggled to keep them dry. The last thing she wanted was to shed angry tears in front of Ashley. It sucked to be mortal right now.

Ashley crossed her arms. "We'll see about that, won't we? Ariel sent two teams on this mission—and we're going to complete the mission—not some half-baked wannabe guardian. I don't know what Ariel was thinking. The legion always gave you far too much credit, if you ask me. The old witch is going to kill you, you know. *I'm* going to get the old hag to help us."

Kara sneered and stepped forward. "Sure you are. Go ahead. Let's see you try—"

"Kara," interrupted David as he pointed to his watch. "I hate to interrupt this lovely cat—fight, but we should get going. It's a twenty minute drive to Boscastle from here, and it's not like we have loads of time."

Kara turned away from Ashley even though she wanted to slap that stuck—up smile off her face permanently. "Yeah...let's go—"

A sudden pain erupted in Kara's head like an explosion. White-hot fire burned her brain. The pain was so intense she wished she could just pass out. A flash of white light burst behind her eyes. She staggered and pressed her hands against her head.

David rushed to her side. "Kara, what is it? What's wrong?" He searched her face.

Kara rubbed her temples.

"It's nothing," she said, feeling the sudden pain lessen and disappear. "Just a massive headache—it's gone now—probably something to do with the pressure from the plane ride. I'm fine—really—don't worry about it. "

The last thing she needed was for them to call off the mission because they thought she might be too fragile.

She felt sudden wetness drip from her nose. And when she reached up and wiped it, red stained her fingers. She frowned as she stared at the blood on her hand. She had never had a nosebleed in her life. She knew David was watching her. She dabbed the blood with a tissue from Mr. Patterson's store. After a moment the blood stopped.

"Kara, you're freaking *bleeding*."

David's expression darkened. "Is that normal for you? Did you used to get them before?"

Kara put the tissue back in her pocket and did her best not to look panicked. "Not really—but it's nothing, look, it's stopped now. It's just a little blood."

David narrowed his eyes. "I have a bad feeling about this, something just doesn't feel right."

Kara felt the strength return to her legs. "David, stop looking at me like I'm about to faint. I'm fine—"

"Didn't look fine from where I am," said Ashley. "Sudden nose bleeds are a bad sign. It looked like you were having a meltdown."

Kara glared at the girl with what she hoped was her best mean face. "I'm not. I'm perfectly fine."

"Oh, but you're not—and that *was* a meltdown." Ashley matched Kara's glare. "You're obviously too weak to finish the mission. It's like I said...you're as good as dead."

David stepped up to Ashley. "Back off air-head. Calling you an idiot would be an insult to all the stupid people."

Ashley laughed softly. "I feel sorry for you David. She's a freak. I'm not alone when I say that she should never have been allowed to join the legion in the first place. You'd be surprised at how many *true* guardians want her gone. She's not truly one of us—and she'll never be. She's tainted. She'll let you down—and bring you all down with her. You're going to fail. Ariel can't trust her. No one can. We're your replacements. We're the backup team."

Jenny stood by Kara's side. "Don't listen to her, Kara—she's full of it. She's just jealous because you're nice and pretty, and she looks like a Pug."

"She's right," said Peter, "she probably envies you, that's why she's being so nasty."

But it was too late. Ashley's words stung. Did Ariel not trust her? Were Ashley and her team here in case she went schizo? Was she meant to fail?

"If you're not back in three hours, we're instructed to go in," said Ashley.

She smiled at Kara. "Good luck, freak." She snapped her fingers and walked away with her goons trotting behind her looking very proud and important.

"That's it," said Jenny. "It's official—I *hate* her." She stuck out her tongue and made a face.

Peter shook his head. "Let's not give her reason to gloat. We need to get a move on."

David eyed Kara carefully. "He's right, we've got to split. Peter, do you know how to get us to Boscastle from here?"

Peter pulled a flat square device that looked like a cell phone from his jacket pocket. He slid his finger across the screen and a small holographic version of a map appeared and hovered in front of him. He waved his hand, and the map disappeared. "Yup. Let's find a cab and get out of here." He pocketed his contraption.

"Forget Ashley," said David, as he watched Kara's face. "It's not true what she said, you know. She's just trying to break you. She wants you to fail. Don't believe her lies."

Kara avoided his eyes. "I don't think all of what she said was lies. Part of me believes her. I see how the other GAs look at me. I'm not blind. I know most of them want me gone."

"We want you with us."

David reached out to take Kara's hand, and she flinched at the sting of current from his touch. "You, Jenny, Peter and me—we're a team. You're one of us."

"No, I'm not—I'm different. I'll never be like you." Kara turned away from David, but not before she saw the pain in his face.

Kara didn't utter a single word during the twenty-minute cab drive to Boscastle village. She sat in the back seat of the dark blue minivan, glaring at her reflection in the window, angry with herself for looking like such a fool in front of Ashley and her entourage. The nosebleed didn't help—but worse was how David was watching her now—like she was about to have a major breakdown at any minute. No one tried to speak to her, and she was very glad, for fear that she might actually have a meltdown.

The drive passed like a blur, and the next thing Kara knew, the minivan had stopped. David paid the driver and everyone climbed out of the car.

They stood in a large parking area overlooking a quaint village with houses painted in every color of the rainbow. The village of Boscastle lay at the foot of three great valleys. To the south, in a deep cleft on the coast, where two deep and steep valleys met the sea, was the harbor. It wended through the valley in the shape of a Z on its way to join the sea. Picturesque boats bobbed on the sheltered water, and a few villagers strolled the streets. A young couple held a map and pointed to one of the houses. Other than that, the village was nearly empty.

Kara's long ponytail flapped in the cool wind, and she was glad of her goose-down coat. Her breath came out in spirals of white steam. The distant smell of fish and seaweed drifted off the ocean.

Jenny pulled her bow from the trunk and swung it over her shoulder. She caught Kara staring. "I know Ariel said our weapons would be useless. I could have been more incognito with just a blade—but I feel naked without my bow, like something's missing. I feel safe and complete with it. And by that look in your eye—you think I'm as crazy as my hair, don't you?"

Kara smiled and shook her head. "Of course not, I know exactly what you mean. And I love your hair."

Kara felt so unprotected without her M-suit. It was like she had jumped into the deepest part of a pool without knowing how to swim. And she was sinking to the bottom.

David smacked his hands together. "Okay, ladies and gents—now that we're here, how about we ask around for the whereabouts of the old bag. I'm sure someone knows where she's hiding."

The early morning sun warmed Kara's face although snow topped the roofs and sprinkled the streets of the little village. Merchants were opening their shops for the day, putting out signs and shoveling the snow from the front doors. A man in his sixties with white hair and trimmed beard was doing some repairs on the nearest cottage. His long green coat flapped in the wind.

"Come on, let's ask him." Kara hurried forward towards the man, the others following at her heels.

The old man looked up as they approached. His weather beaten face broke into a wide grin. "Visitors, eh? What can I do for you on this cold morning? Can I offer you some breakfast?"

Kara smiled. "No thank you. Uh...we were wondering if you..." she faltered. She knew how crazy it was going to sound asking about a witch, but she had to try. She said, "Could tell us where the witch Olga lives?"

The old man's smile disappeared, and he blanched. He eyed Jenny's bow suspiciously and frowned. "I don't know no witch. I don't know where you tourists get your crazy ideas. Leave me alone."

He turned, headed quickly back inside his cottage, and slammed the door shut with a *bang*.

"Nice," said David as he laughed. "I was looking forward to some breakfast. Nothing like fat juicy sausages, bacon, and pancakes to start the day. Man, those were the days..."

"Did you see how scared he was when you mentioned the witch's name?" said Jenny. She glanced back at the old man's cottage. "It's like he froze up or something."

"Yeah, he totally spazed," agreed Peter, and he examined the street. "At least we know we're in the right place—we should definitely try someone else."

Kara sighed and looked across the street. A young woman in her twenties was adjusting Christmas lights and red Christmas bows around a small shop's bay window. She wore a tomato-red coat, and her silky raven hair fluttered in the wind. The words, *Margaret's Marvels*, were etched in red on the glass.

"Well, maybe this lady knows." Kara jogged across the street towards the shop.

"Excuse me," said Kara with the best smile she could muster. "We're looking for a woman named Olga." She figured she would leave the witch part out this time. "Do you know where she lives? We really need to speak to her—it's important."

But it was no use. The woman's eyes widened and she ran back inside her shop and flipped the sign to *CLOSED*.

"What did you do to her?" David ran to Kara's side, a wide grin spread on his face. "The last time a girl ran away from me like that was because I—"

Kara shoved David. "Spare us the details, lover boy. We need to find the old witch. Someone's got to help us. Someone has to know where she lives!" She threw up her hands.

"Well, I don't think the villagers are going to help. Look." Peter cocked his head towards the street. Kara saw frightened faces behind the windows. They shut the blinds and pulled the curtains shut all along the street. The villagers were shutting them out.

"I'm guessing they don't like the witch," said Jenny.

"Maybe she tried to eat their children," offered David innocently. "Have you thought about that? Maybe that's what the witches do here—kid-stew."

"Peter, you wouldn't happen to have a witch-GPS on you?" Kara was desperate.

Peter shrugged. "No, sorry. I wish I did though—it'll take all day to try and look for her on our own. She could be anywhere, and we don't have much time."

"You don't have to remind me." Kara's nerves were shot, and what was worse, her head started to throb again. The ground shifted, and she fought a sudden dizzy spell. They were getting worse. She focused on finding the witch.

When Ariel had said the villagers would know where to look for the witch, she hadn't anticipated this kind of hostility. Kara looked beyond the village. A vast cliff stood at the edge of the village. She could just make out a small path leading into it.

David danced on the spot and looked pleased with himself. "Our luck has changed, mates."

He pointed to a dingy old pub nestled between two cottages. "There's nothing that can quench a thirst, like a chilled lager on a cold day. My prayers have been answered—and it's a *pub*." He started to walk, but Kara pulled him back.

"You're underage, dummy. You can't just walk in there."

"Guys! Look!" said Peter, pointing.

Next to David's pub was a small shop made of grey stone with black shutters. A small black sign with white painted letters read, *Feats or Tricks, Witchcraft Depot.*

David whistled loudly. "Well, if *they* can't help us find the witch Olga, then I'm a friggin' monkey."

Kara couldn't believe their luck. There was only one way to find out if they were right.

"Come on." Forgetting the pounding pain in her head, she sprinted to the large black door with peeling paint. A witch's mask was carved out of the door. The handle sprouted out of the witch's mouth like a warped tongue. Kara grabbed the cool handle and pushed in.

A wind chime rang as the door swung open. The air was hot with the smell of incense. Kara's throat burned right away and she began to cough again.

"Whoa...would you look at this place." David's jaw dropped. "It's awesome. I feel like we've just stepped in a haunted fun house."

Kara wiped the water from her eyes and looked around.

The tiny shop was cluttered with witchcraft merchandise. Hundreds of cauldrons were stacked on top of each other and grazed the ceiling in topsy-turvy columns. Dolls with red eyes made of straw, pitchforks, brooms of every size and color of straw, medallions, necklaces, crystal balls, and even sharp daggers carved like claws filled the counters and shelves. The soft yellow light that lit the store came from scores of candles that hung from the walls on iron sconces in the shape of eyes. Incense burned in a burner in the shape of a horned god. A large medallion with a spiral symbol etched into the metal hung from a nail on the sidewall.

Kara suddenly felt eyes on the back of her head. She turned sideways. Three black cats lay lazily across a counter on the far left of the shop. Their smooth ebony fur glistened in the soft light like liquid tar. They watched Kara with yellow eyes. Something brushed her ankles—another black cat swerved between her legs. With its tail in the air, it walked calmly away and disappeared behind stacks of boxes at the back of the store.

"Oh. My. God. Aren't they beautiful? I love cats." Jenny leaned on the counter and reached out her hand towards one of the cats. The cat bared its teeth and spat at her aggressively. In a flash, it slashed her with its paw and ripped the sleeve on her jacket. Jenny cursed loudly and pulled her hand away.

"Not so pretty anymore, are they?" David and Peter exchanged a look and started laughing.

Jenny lowered her eyes. She turned to make sure the boys weren't looking, and in one swift movement she pushed the cat off the counter. "Scram. That was my favorite jacket, fur ball."

Kara laughed. Just then she noticed a wooden sign hanging next to the counter. The sign read:

Warning to all thieves:

Take without paying and be cursed!

It occurred to Kara that perhaps the owner was a witch. What if this was Olga's shop? If it were, she would have a bit more time to convince her. She thought about how her speech would go. *Hi, I'm a guardian—please don't kill us.*

"Hey guys, come check this out," called David from the back of the store. "You won't believe it."

Jenny smiled, and they both walked over to David and Peter. Their foreheads were pressed against a large glass wall—their eyes glued to something on the other side. Kara moved closer for a better look. Behind the glass wall was an assortment of metal shackles. An engraved metal plate was fastened to the glass wall. The inscription read:

WD Number: 1677

Object Name: Shackle

Classification: Persecution/Torture

Information: Early waist band used in the torture of witches during the 16th and 17th centuries

The hairs on the back of Kara's neck stood up. "You think those things are real?" She remembered reading about the torture of witches in the 16th centuries. It made her sick how quickly people back then had accused women of witchcraft, blaming them for their crops going bad or the lack of rain. Women were even blamed for the death of newborns. In the 16th century, Kara would have burned as a witch.

"They've gotta be real," said David. "I don't think they'd be protected behind this glass if they weren't. My guess is that they're *very* real."

Kara swallowed. Maroon stains spotted the shackles, and her stomach gave a lurch. "Is that—is that blood?"

Peter lowered his head. "Looks like it, but it could be just dirt," he added quickly when he noticed Kara's face. "Yeah—I'm sure it's just dirt."

He gave David a worried look.

Despite the dry, hot shop, Kara shivered. She stared at the shackles, feeling cold and disgusted. What kind of witch would put them up for display? Unconsciously, she fiddled with her leather bracelet and wondered how those cold shackles would feel against her skin.

"This is seriously sick, if they're real," said Jenny, preoccupied with the shackles. "It's gotta be a joke, or just a hoax to attract more tourists to this lame town—"

"I can assure you that this is no joke," said a raspy voice behind them.

Kara whirled around. Her breath caught in her throat.

The weirdest thing she had ever seen stepped from the shadows. Connected at the waist were the ugliest Siamese twins she had ever seen.

CHAPTER 7

MS. FAY AND MS. FAY

THE SIAMESE TWINS LOOKED like a four-legged human spider. They shuffled forward, and Kara took an unconscious step back and hit her head on the glass wall. They were dressed exactly the same, in a black suit and tie. They looked like dreary funeral parlor directors with haunted expressions. Their heads were large and oblong, and their haggard faces drooped with wrinkles that made their wet eyes look unnaturally large. Both had raven colored hair that hung in greasy clumps and was cut straight across their jaws. Their eyes and eyebrows were unevenly lined in black kohl, as if they had put on their makeup in the dark.

One of the twins was slightly shorter, and her head hung unnaturally sideways, as though her neck had been broken. She sucked desperately on a cigarette, like it was oxygen, and then her sister opened her mouth and exhaled puffs of white smoke.

Their yellow eyes brightened at the sight of Kara and her friends, just like the cats.

"Look here, sister," said the taller woman. Remnants of the cigarette smoke escaped her lips and her voice was rough as though she was suffering from a severe case of strep throat.

"We have ourselves some visitors. Young, by the looks of them."

Her sister smiled and revealed a mouth full of rotten yellow teeth. She looked as if she had smoked over a million cigarettes, and toothpaste hadn't been invented yet. She took another long haul of her cigarette.

"Yes, sister, four of them...but these are not *ordinary* visitors," she answered in an identical raspy voice. "No, these visitors are *altered*—disguised as the living—very unnatural."

"Yes, sister, very unnatural. Why would the walking dead, s*pirit walkers*, dare to enter our establishment? Not the cleverest of abominations to come here, where the dead are not welcome."

"Indeed, you are right to ask, sister. Except for one."

"Yes, sister, except for one."

The shorter woman lifted her head, closed her eyes for a moment and sniffed the air.

"I can smell it on her, sweet like candy and dandelion syrup. Hmm—very strange for one so young, but it's there all right, and no mistake."

Her eyes popped open suddenly, and she shook her head looking disappointed.

"You keep very strange company little girl," she said, her eerie yellow eyes focused on Kara. "It is very odd that someone like *you*, should be with the likes of *them*. Are you aware of what company you keep? Do you know what these creatures are? They are abominations walking the Earth. Very unnatural—and a threat to the world of the living."

Kara shifted uneasily on the spot, but she stood her ground, determined not to let those eyes creep her out. There was something very odd about those yellow eyes. It was almost as though they could see things that other mortals could not. Could they see through the M-suits?

"I feel like I'm in the twilight zone," whispered David in Kara's ear. "Look at them. I'm going to have nightmares for years—mark my words."

The twins' eyes widened, and they shuffled with surprising speed towards David. They glared at him with their hands on their hips and measured him like he was a curious object. Their yellow eyes glistened.

The shorter twin pointed a bone-thin finger with a long dirty nail at David. "You must knock on wood three times after mentioning cruel words, or the evil spirits will ruin things for you, *spirit walker*," she said and then sucked on her cigarette.

David lifted his hands in surrender. "Uh...sure...right, whatever you say."

The other twin blew what looked like a broomstick made of smoke in David's face.

"You spirits who walk the Earth would be wise to hold your tongues in the presence of the Fay sisters. We have lived with your spiteful remarks all our lives. But despite how you perceive us, *we* are not unnatural. *You* are."

David shared a look with Kara that said, *what the*—and she could tell he was straining to keep from laughing out loud. She knew he couldn't keep his mouth shut for long. This was going to end badly if she didn't intervene. Jenny and Peter both looked at Kara and shrugged, they seemed to be waiting for her to do something.

"I beg your pardon, Miss Fay," said Kara to the shorter twin, "and to you Miss Fay," she said to the other, "my friend didn't mean what he said, and he is very sorry. Aren't you David?"

When he didn't answer, she kicked him.

"Uh...yes, yes, of course," David tried to compose himself. He pressed his hand to his chest and said with fake humility. "I apologize. I am deeply ashamed and grief-stricken for the pain I have caused to such *admirable* women."

The Fay sisters scowled at David. Their ugly faces twisted even more. They stared at the group intensely, their wet yellow eyes never blinking.

"Why are you here, spirit walkers?" asked the shorter sister. "Why have you spoiled our shop with your corrupted presence? It'll take all day to wash your scum from our floors. You shouldn't be here."

Her warm putrid breath reached Kara's nose, and she took another haul of her cigarette.

David smiled innocently. "I thought we could borrow those handcuffs over there for a game of—ouch!" He cried out and rubbed his shoulder.

Kara shook her fist at him. "Stop being an idiot! We don't have time."

She looked over to Peter and Jenny who looked as annoyed by David's reaction as Kara had been. Jenny rolled her eyes and Peter avoided David's triumphant expression.

The taller Miss Fay blew an impressive cat-shape smoke silhouette in the air.

"Why have you come to seek the wisdom of the Fay sisters, spirit walkers? I doubt you're seriously interested in our merchandise. Spirit walkers don't mingle with witchcraft—unless we are mistaken. Are you here to purchase a cauldron, perhaps?"

The old woman wheezed as she tried to laugh. She started to cough, and her sister smacked her on the back until the woman coughed up some phlegm and spat it out on the ground near David's feet. He jumped back just in time as the green gunk hit the floor.

"Why are you calling us spirit walkers?" asked Kara, as she pulled her eyes away from the greenish slime on the ground. "What does that mean exactly?"

The taller sister scratched the top of her greasy head and flicked off what Kara hoped was just dandruff.

"*They...*" she pointed slowly to David, Jenny and Peter, "are spirit walkers, spirits of the dead in mortal bodies. They are as unnatural as they come, a *disgusting* corruption of nature. Our mother earth is a world for the living—not the dead. They are nature's enemy—therefore they are *our* enemy. They should not be."

"Look who's talking," mumbled Jenny. She lowered her eyes and crossed her arms over her chest. She looked prepared for a fight. Kara had never seen her look so angry.

"But you, little one, you are not one of them," continued the old woman. Her yellow eyes fixed on Kara once more. "And yet, there is something different in you—something *special*."

Kara frowned, feeling uncomfortable. "So, obviously you know they're supernatural beings. You can see through their M-suits."

"Of course we can, we are the Fay sisters," chorused the twins looking very pleased with themselves.

Kara wasn't sure what they meant by that. But something nagged her. Those unsettling yellow eyes...

"So then—I'm guessing you're witches, aren't you?" she asked. "You have to be. Regular mortals couldn't see past the M-suits."

The Fay sisters both smiled, showing rows of rotten teeth. They tried to turn their heads to look at each other, but only got halfway.

"Clever, that one," said the shorter sister. "Of course we are witches."

She pulled another cigarette from her jacket pocket. With a flick of her hand, a flame sprouted from her fingertips, and the witch sucked on her cigarette happily as though it were a lollypop.

Kara felt relieved—two witches were better than one. The Fay sisters would help them destroy the dark warlock. She was certain they were the ones Ariel called dark witches. What better to fight off a dark warlock than a couple of dark witches who just happened to be stuck together by the hip? Perhaps they were stronger that way, witch magic to the power of two.

A smile materialized on Peter's pale face, and Jenny almost seemed pleased, although she kept glaring at the witches. David raised his brows as he met Kara's eyes, a smile twitched on his lips.

Kara bounced on the spot. "Thank God. Listen, you have to help us. We need your help to vanquish a dark warlock. I'm sure you know all about warlocks—see, he's stealing souls from mortals, and he's going to perform a ritual on the winter solstice that will kill thousands of innocent mortals—"

"We cannot help you," chorused the witches.

"But..." Kara watched the witches in disbelief. "Please—you don't understand. My...my mother's been infected by his dark magic. She's dying. We need your magic to destroy him. Our weapons are useless against him. Your magic is our only chance. Please." Kara started to sweat. A cat jumped from a top shelf onto the tallest sister's right shoulder. Intelligence flashed in its yellow eyes. The old witch stroked the cat as she spoke. "I'm sorry, but we cannot help you, child."

"Why?" said Kara, her voice rising with her temper. "You would be helping thousands of innocent people. I'm sure you want to do the right thing, don't you? You wouldn't want innocent people killed, right?"

"You don't understand," said the witch. "It's not that we don't want to help you..."

"...we *can't* help you," finished her twin sister as she took a drag from her cigarette.

Kara felt the blood drain from her face. The words wouldn't come.

"Why not?" said Jenny, in a voice that matched her scowl. "You're obviously witches—you have magic fingers. We just saw you do magic. I know you hate us *spirit walkers*, you made that obvious, but you'd be helping the mortals. Don't you want help them?"

The short witch flicked the ashes from her cigarette on Jenny's boots, sneering at her like Jenny was some sort of ugly insect.

"Our magic is limited, spirit walker. We can make fire...cast a few spells. We can even make love potions for the desperate lover, but that is all."

She raised her arms in the air. "This is why we have this establishment. We are more businesswomen than actual witches. We do not possess the necessary skills that you are looking for."

"It takes a very powerful witch to bring down a warlock," said the taller sister. "One with old magic—dark magic—a sorceress skilled in the dark arts. There is only one witch who possesses the knowledge and ancient wisdom of the dark arts. All the creatures of the earth and of the spirit world fear her. She is the only one who holds the power to destroy your warlock."

Both women stared intensely at Kara. It was almost as if they wanted her to guess the answer. And Kara had already guessed.

"Olga," she said, and the witches seemed pleased. "You know where she is, don't you? If she's the only one who can help us, then I need to know where she is," she demanded.

The sisters smiled, as if this was a game to them. "She lives in the deep, darkest part of Shadow Cave," chorused the twins.

"Sounds spooky," whispered David. "I'm tingling all over."

"You must leave the village and go south," said the shorter twin. "Follow the red path down past the harbor and continue down the cliff. And at the edge of the cliff where the ocean meets rock, is where you will find Shadow Cave. You will see a break in the cliff, and that is where you can enter."

The witch raised her skeletal finger in Kara's face. "You must keep to the path once you're in the cave. Do not stray from the path."

Kara gagged as the woman's rancid breath shot up her nose.

"Why not?" asked David. "I was a boy scout once—I'm pretty sure I can find our way back."

"Dark things live in Shadow Cave," said the witch.

She kept her focus on Kara as though the others weren't important. "Creatures from the depths of darkness will drink your blood and eat your soul if you stray from the path. You must never leave the path! The path will lead you to the witch—amongst other things..."

"Sounds easy enough," said David. "Just follow the path. Let's get to it—"

The witches pointed crooked fingers at David, then at Jenny and Peter.

"*You* spirit walkers cannot enter Shadow Cave. It is forbidden. Only natural living creatures can enter. And even then, they might not make it out alive. Many mortals have ventured into the cave and have never been seen again. You are taking a great risk just to step foot into this cave. This quest you're on, it better be worth risking your life."

Kara's sudden burst of triumph was deflating rapidly. It wasn't going to be as easy as she first thought. If the others couldn't come with her...

"So what happens if we do enter," asked Peter politely. "We won't disturb anything, I promise, we only seek help."

The witches turned on him. "Unnatural creatures like you will be destroyed," said the taller sister while the other sucked on her cigarette once more. "The cave will sense it. It will want to protect itself from your *abnormality*. It will see you as a threat, a foreign entity, and it will kill you. And if the cave doesn't destroy, then the witch Olga will. She has killed many spirit walkers before. If you dare to enter, then prepare yourselves, spirit walkers, to meet your doom." Their yellow eyes focused on Kara. "Only *she* can enter."

David paced on the spot. "We're angels, ladies, and we're not afraid of any big spooky cave or an old hag. We're going with Kara to see the old witch and nothing's going to stop us."

He stood with his hands clenched into fists, daring the twins to say anything.

The shorter sister flicked her cigarette to the floor and squished it with her pointy black leather boot.

"We sense something in you," she said, looking at Kara and ignoring David completely. "We see a special aura around you. It's powerful, but we don't know what it is. It hides from us, and we don't have the talent to see more."

"Like a light," said the other sister. "That switches on and off."

"Perhaps you might live—after all. Perhaps the witch Olga will let you live."

"Jeez. Thanks for the vote of confidence." Kara sighed.

She felt worse than ever and looked at her friends. "We should get going. It's quite the hike up the hill, and I'm just a mortal. I don't have a special suit."

"I can carry you if you want." David flashed his usual smile. "I don't mind, fair lady."

"I'm sure you don't."

Kara looked to the witches. "Um, thank you for your...help."

"We hope you find what you are seeking, child," said the taller witch as she stroked the cat's head. It closed its eyes and purred loudly. "You should take care of those nose bleeds."

"Huh?" Kara reached for her nose, it was bleeding again.

The taller sister pulled out a yellow handkerchief with the initials *F.S.* etched in black and gave it to her.

"Well, you have a...lovely shop," Kara said awkwardly, pressing the handkerchief against her nose, "but we really must be leaving now." She offered back the handkerchief that was now stained with blood, but the twins waved her off.

"Keep it," they said together. "Good bye."

"Good bye." Kara pocketed the handkerchief.

They all walked out the front door, anxious to get out of the stuffy store and away from the Siamese twins' hypnotic yellow eyes. Kara stepped into the street and gladly gulped down buckets of fresh air.

"Good luck, spirit walkers," laughed the twins from the threshold of their store. "Don't say we didn't warn you. Prepare to die."

CHAPTER 8

WATER SURPRISE

AFTER JENNY HAD THROWN every curse in the *Book of Curses* at the Fay sisters, the sisters slammed the shop's door in Jenny's face. Kara and her team left the little village and headed south towards the harbor.

The harbor lay between two giant masses of rock that meandered out into the ocean. As soon as they put the quaint cottages behind them, a narrow path of stone stretched out before them and snaked down along the edge of a three-hundred foot cliff. And somewhere below the cliff lay Shadow Cave. Even from the distance Kara could sense a presence about that cliff, something unnatural and dark.

Frost covered the wild flowers and dense shrubs that lined the path on either side. The cold air made every breath harder on her lungs. She was determined to make it to the bottom without stopping to catch her breath. Without her elemental power, she was nothing more than a little mortal girl, a weakling with nosebleeds.

Kara's leg muscles strained as she climbed down the winding path. She did her best to match the others' pace down the hill, but they were like robots, supernatural machines that never showed any sign of fatigue. Her puny little chicken-legs were no match for their powerful M-5 suits.

A pulsing pain began to throb against the back of her eyeballs. She rubbed her temples and did her best to hide the pain. She pressed on like a good little soldier and hoped she wouldn't get another nosebleed.

"I hope I never see those ugly twins ever again," said Jenny as she marched purposefully down the hill.

"I bet they lied to us. I have a feeling they're sending us into a trap. It was obvious they hated us, *spirit walkers*. I mean, we're the good guys, and they still treated us like dirt."

"It wouldn't surprise me if it were a trap," agreed Peter. "I couldn't help but feel creeped out by them—and those weird yellow eyes? What was up with that?"

Jenny's voice rose. "Calling us abominations, unnatural! I'll show them what's unnatural with my boot up their—"

"Ugh! I don't want to think about what they might—" said Peter, with a twisted expression like he just bit into something sour.

David threw up his hands. "—too late! I've already damaged my virgin mind with a mental image of their butts."

"Can we talk about something else, please?" said Kara, a little out of breath.

David jogged over to Kara's side.

"Are you doing all right? You know, my offer of a ride still stands if you want—I don't mind."

In the sun, his skin sparkled as though it was painted with liquid diamonds. His arm brushed up against hers, and a spark vibrated inside her. He smiled; his lips were just too perfect, too close...

Kara looked away as blood rushed to her face. "No, I'm fine, but thanks. I think I can manage the rest of the way without one of my lungs collapsing. It can't be much further."

She hoped she sounded convincing enough, and that it was just the long walk that was responsible for her flushed face.

"My sole life's purpose is to please your, ladyship," said David, his eyes twinkled. "I am at your disposal," he bowed very low, and Kara heard Peter snort.

Kara smiled slowly, and she felt her ears going hot. "Don't make me laugh. It's hard enough without laughing. I need all my strength to keep going down this hill without falling over," she said in rapid breaths.

David stared at her for a moment. His smile disappeared. "I hope the legion knows what they're doing—sending you in as a mortal." He searched the shoreline below as they walked.

Kara didn't answer. She was wondering the same thing.

She searched his face. It was strange having David the angel beside her when she was a mortal. They had fought together, side by side as GAs, their friendship growing tighter with every new mission. Their special bond was unbreakable. She knew he would give up his soul for her, and she would do the same.

And as mortals, she and David had begun a life together. It had felt natural. But now she felt more unsure of herself and nervous around him. She wasn't sure how to act with David anymore. Even with the memories, it was almost like the first time they met. Her heart hammered at her chest whenever their eyes met. Was this because she was mortal now? She felt confused, her feelings blocked. She wondered if her doubts were an after effect of the memory projection. Maybe the oracles had damaged her somehow. It would explain the headaches and nosebleeds— and the lack of energy.

After an hour descending the valley, they had made it to the edge of the cliff. Kara cradled the cramp in her side and looked around over the edge. Her hair and jacket flapped in the strong wind. The great blue ocean spread out below them. Massive waves crashed onto the rocks below.

She could see a zigzag flight of wet stone steps that had been cut into the stone and followed a steep descent to a small patch of golden sand. It was about a hundred and fifty feet down from the top of the steps, and each step was coated with a deadly combination of slippery green moss and snow. A shadow passed down the cliff, and Kara looked to the sky. The sun had disappeared under a layer of dark grey clouds that had moved in on them with unnatural speed. The winds intensified. She had the feeling someone was watching them.

David stood next to her. "You want us to take a few minutes break so that you can catch your breath?"

Kara shook her hot face and wiped the sweat from her forehead.

"No, I'm fine," she lied. Her head spun as she hyperventilated.

"Going down is easy, but the climb back up will be a challenge."

She wondered if she'd survive the cave—to make the trip back up. She saw David and Jenny share a look, but they said nothing.

She wanted to rest until she could breathe normally, but she refused to show them how weak she was. She could see their doubts in their eyes. They didn't believe she could do the mission either—their doubt inspired her to prove them wrong.

"There's only one way to find out where these stairs lead. Come on, let's go say hi to Olga." She walked around the edge of the cliff, and the blood began to flow back into her cramped up legs.

David examined the stone stairway and whistled loudly. "That's a lot of steps. You sure you can handle it?"

"I'm sure."

Kara didn't wait for David to respond. She climbed down the slippery steps carefully, one at a time. She knew that one wrong move—and she'd be doing a double-dive into the freezing ocean below. David's boots clomped behind her, and she could hear Jenny arguing with Peter as they made their descent.

Icy winds pushed against Kara, almost knocking her sideways. Debris and snow flapped against her face. Her foot slipped, but she steadied herself. She squinted into the storm. It was as though the winds didn't want them to go down. Was the wind protecting them—or trying to kill them. Was this part of the old witch's magic? Could her magic reach as far as the cliffs?

Halfway down the steps, Kara was shivering and sweaty. It was so steep that she could press her uphill hand against the rocky ledge for support the rest of the way down. Another strong gust of wind struck her as if giant invisible hands were pushing it. The clouds were getting thicker and darker. Someone or something didn't want them here—

Her feet slipped, but as she started to slide down the wet stairs towards the cliff, she felt a strong hold on her arm. Through the gusts of sand, sea, and snow she could make out David's silhouette.

"What's happening," she yelled through the wind. "It's like the wind doesn't want us here?"

"I have no idea," yelled David. "It's getting worse—we better hurry and get down."

Kara didn't like the sound of that. If she went any faster, she'd slip and keel over into the sea. Determined, she stepped down carefully and descended the slippery stones as fast as she could. The feeling of being watched settled over her again. She looked up.

Grey tornados the size of a garage sped towards them. At the last minute they shifted course and dove into the sea below. The water's surface bubbled and white foam formed on the top. Suddenly, a pair of giant arms made of seawater sprouted from the ocean below, as though the god of the sea was reaching out to them with giant semitransparent gloves. Water rolled off them in never-ending waterfalls.

"What the heck are those?" cried David through the storm.

Kara didn't answer. Paralyzed, she stared as the enormous hands the size of SUVs curled their fingers and formed two massive fists.

Like water hammers, the fists came crashing down on them.

Kara leaped sideways. The fist missed her by an inch and left her drenched in seawater. Then she saw Peter flatten himself against the cliff's ledge just in time to avoid being smashed by the other fist. Water splashed against his glasses, as the fist collapsed back into water. But the water rolled back together, like molecules forming something solid.

As the hands reformed, David jumped forward and swung at the first fist. His blade passed easily through the water—with no effect. The hand seemed to crack its knuckles in response to David's attempt.

"It was worth a try." David looked at Kara and shrugged.

Together, the colossal arms lifted and swayed backwards as they prepared for another deadly blow.

"If they knock us down into the ocean," yelled David, "—you're a goner. Our mortal bodies will disintegrate, and we'll be back in Horizon, but you'll be alone. I can't let that happen, not when we're so close."

Kara narrowed her eyes—she knew it was true.

But the hands came together, turned upside down and formed a mouth and eyes with their fingers, like a shadow puppet. The mouth moved, and a voice thundered all around.

"Go back, spirit walkers, or your souls will be mine!"

"Fantastic," said David, "talking giant hands, that's all we needed."

He waved his own fist at the giant water-arms. "How about you cut us some slack? Hey, man! Manicures don't exist in your size—it's not our fault!"

"You've been warned!" boomed the voice.

The wind picked up with a vengeance. The entire cliff trembled as rock and sand rained down on them. Kara's jacket flapped madly in the wind. Her wet hair slapped her face, and she had to squat to keep her balance. Shivering in the cold, her face burned with every gust of icy wind. If the giant fists didn't kill her, then she'd die of pneumonia.

Jenny and Peter screamed.

A giant fist came plummeting at them. Miraculously, they jumped out of the way just in time. The fist crashed into the side of the cliff like a giant exploding water balloon.

The other fist came straight for Kara.

She didn't even have time to blink as the giant water fist soared towards her. She leaped, but she wasn't fast enough. The great water fist crashed into the side of her leg. She screamed, lost her grip, and fell.

Sharp rock scraped her face as she smashed and slid down the cliff. Rocks and boulders raced past her and wind howled in her ears. She flailed out her arms and legs—desperately grasping for something to hold on to. She felt like she had been falling for minutes.

Her boots found a small ledge and stopped her fall. Stinging with pain, she grabbed hold of a crevice with her bloodied fingers. She hung on by her fingertips and toes. Adrenaline pulsed through her body. Her heart thundered against her chest—she dared not look down.

"Kara!" David called above the wailing winds. "Don't move. I'm coming down."

She looked up—she had fallen at least thirty feet.

She turned her face towards the sea—another water-fist came at her.

She rolled to the side.

SMASH!

Seawater exploded on her back, and knocked the air out of her. It was like being hit by a tidal wave. The cliff itself shook under the impact. Kara was drenched.

Then her fingers slipped, and she fell.

CHAPTER 9

SHADOW CAVE

*T*HIS IS IT, KARA thought. *I'm dead.*

Wind whistled in her ears as she fell. The side of her face scraped against the razor sharp rock. She knew she shouldn't fear death like a normal person would, but she did—her instinct to survive was strong even though death seemed inevitable.

She counted in her head.

One...

Kara crashed onto something pillow soft. She spat the dirt from her mouth and sat up.

"I'm alive?"

She looked at her bloodied hands. They stung like she had soaked them in acid, but blood meant life. She was alive. A little banged up, but alive. Apart from a small strain in her foot, she seemed fine. She was sitting in a bed of moss and stringy coastal vegetation. It had saved her. Sharp boulders lay to her left. If she had fallen another few feet to the left she would have been human-mush.

Kara examined the cliff above her. It looked like a regular cliff, made mostly of jagged rock with a few spurts of vegetation in the crevices. The base of the cliff disappeared into the ocean. Great ocean waves smashed onto the rocks on the north side of the cliff. But she had landed near a small semicircle patch of golden sand sheltered under the cliff. And at the edge of the sand, was an opening—just as the Fay sisters had said—the entrance to Shadow Cave was a perfect triangle like an upside-down piece of pie. Was it a death wish that drew her towards the mouth of the cave? Only shadows lingered beyond the narrow opening. Something was watching her from inside the cave—she could feel it.

David charged down the steps at a frightening speed. He jumped the last step and landed softly by Kara.

"Kara! Are you all right? Are you hurt?"

Kara took his hand, and he pulled her up. "Call it a miracle, but I'm fine." Her ankle throbbed and she adjusted her weight on the other foot. "I think I sprained my ankle."

"You have cuts on your face." David squeezed her arm and didn't let her go. "They're bleeding—"

"Watch out! They're coming!"

Peter and Jenny came crashing down the last steps but managed to stay on their feet. Kara looked up. Seawater dripped on her face like an outdoor shower. The sea-fists hovered above the cliff for a moment and then plummeted towards them like giant water grenades.

Kara pointed towards the cave. "RUN!"

Jenny and Peter dashed towards the cave. David pulled Kara with him. The ground shook as the first fist hit the ground where Kara had stood seconds before. The impact of the blow sent them sprawling. The second fist came at them with a vengeance, as if it could see they were getting away.

Just as it hit, David pulled Kara out of the way. The water-fist exploded in a great wave that pushed them like body-surfers all the way to the entrance of the cave. As the water receded, Kara was dragged back towards the deep water.

With lightning speed David hauled Kara out of the water, and they tumbled through the entrance of the cave.

Even in the darkness, Kara could see David's smiling face. She pushed herself up and turned towards the opening. "They're gone."

"For now," said David. "I don't want to be here when they decide to come back."

"You guys all right?" asked Kara, seeing the whites of Jenny and Peter's eyes in the darkness.

"As all right as we can be," answered Peter with his back pressed against the wall of the cave.

Jenny wiped herself down. "I've never seen anything like those giant hands before. You think they had something to do with the witch?"

Kara nodded. "I'm sure of it. Olga doesn't want us here."

"You mean us *spirit walkers*," said Peter.

Kara didn't answer as she inspected the inside of the cave. It was shaped like a pear. The walls came together gradually and disappeared into the blackness above. Icicle-shaped formations drooped from the ceilings and stood up from the floor of the cave. Multicolored mushrooms spread on the ground like bumpy grass, and seeping water covered the walls like sheets of a waterfall. The only source of light came from the entrance.

They stood in a small oval-shaped underground chamber the size of a large room. Thick roots covered the inside walls like cobwebs, and the cave walls shook under the relentless pounding of the waves outside.

On the opposite side was a large crack. Kara stepped towards the fracture in the cave wall and peered through it. She could see a network of underground passages that disappeared into shadows. Somewhere down there was the witch, Olga. Kara couldn't see the roof of the cave in the darkness above her. Humming that sounded like a cross between a motor running and a language came from the deep. Goosebumps rippled across Kara's skin.

"I'm sure we haven't seen the last of what the witch can do. Must be loads of creatures deep in here," said David as he peeled purple moss off the side of the cave wall.

"Anyone up for a stroll in the cave," he said and crossed the chamber. "Well, I am. Let's show these Fay sisters that we angels aren't afraid of the dark."

"Did you guys feel that?" Jenny looked over to Kara, her green eyes wide with fear.

David shrugged. "I don't feel anything?"

Jenny edged back. "That humming—it's like the cave's telling us to get out."

"I'm feeling that, too." Peter was glued to the side of the cave. "It doesn't like us, it's telling us to go back."

"I feel it, too," said Kara.

A shadow moved in the darkness beyond—a bat maybe?

"But it's not like I have a choice. If you guys want to go back, I'll understand. I won't force you to come with me. You heard what the witches said—"

"No way, Kara," said Jenny. "You heard what Ariel said too. We're here to protect you. We go with you, those are our orders."

Peter nodded in agreement.

David pulled a soul blade from his jacket pocket and handed it to Kara. "I know our weapons don't work against warlocks and magic, but I'd feel better if you had one with you, just in case."

Kara wrapped her hand around the hilt of the small blade. It felt awkward and heavy in her hand, not at all like the lightness and balance of her blade when she was a guardian. Could she even use it properly?

"Thanks," she said. "I guess I can hack some stalactites if they try to attack me."

"Stay close to me." David was serious. "You're not in an M-suit like us—whatever's in there is not friendly, and I don't want you getting hurt."

Kara's insides fluttered, and she stiffened with courage. "I'm not that useless, I still remember how to fight. Besides, I'm more worried about you guys than me. Remember what the witches said, *spirit walkers* are not welcome in this cave. Olga isn't going to roll out the red carpet for you. I might have a better chance on my own—"

"Forget it," said David. "Besides, I think those two old bats smoke too much. It's just a cave, what could happen?" he said with a coy smile.

Kara glanced at her watch. It was twenty past noon. Time was running out. "Let's go find this witch and hope she's happy to see us."

But Kara very much doubted that. She had a feeling it was going to take a miracle to convince the old witch Olga. And Kara didn't have a get-a-miracle-free card with her.

David climbed through the crack first, followed closely by Kara with Jenny and Peter bringing up the rear. Immediately, Kara understood the meaning of the cave's name. Twenty feet into the first passageway, and Shadow Cave was as dark as night. She waited for her eyes to get adjusted to the blackness, but it was useless. It was pitch black and as silent as a tomb. The world outside was shut out.

Kara unzipped her jacket. The thick air was humid, and it was surprisingly warm. She smelled earth and limestone.

"Uh...guys? Who turned off the lights," Jenny's voice called out in the darkness.

David held a moonstone the size of a grapefruit in front of him with one hand and brandished his blade in the other. The glow of light illuminated the underground passageway and bathed David in a soft white light. Peter brandished another, and between their two moonstones there was enough light to see the network of passages more clearly.

They stood in the largest of the underground passages that they could see. Smaller passages branched off in every direction. A thick mist coiled around Kara's boots and covered the path in white.

"Which way do we go?"

David cast a long black shadow as he explored the path by the light of his moonstone.

"Let's keep on this one. I think it's the path the clown sisters talked about. It's the largest one—we should follow it."

"Okay." Kara saw movement in the corner of her eye. She turned but could see nothing in the black passageway.

Jenny slid her bow off her shoulders and nocked a silver arrow.

"Something's watching us," she whispered and stared at the passages to her left. "I saw something moving in there." Jenny eyed the cave walls suspiciously.

Kara felt a shiver pass through her. She also felt watched. She strained through the thick darkness and tightened her grip on her blade, but it was impossible to see without night vision. She took a step forward and listened—

Suddenly the ground shifted and trembled. The cave cracked like lightning.

All around them, gigantic mushrooms the size of fridges sprouted from the ground and walls of the cave. They looked like a cross between a humanoid and a vegetable, with long gangly limbs and roots that looked like fingers and toes. They appeared to be eyeless. Their skin was rough like tree bark, and their colors ranged from bright red to forest green.

They lowered their caps, as though they were going to curtsy, and revealed maws of razor sharp teeth on top of their heads. They slithered across the path and created an impenetrable wall of twisted roots and limbs.

David whistled loudly. "Got to admit, the witch has a wicked sense of humor."

A thick mushroom thrashed forward and swung its limbs violently towards David's head. He ducked out of the way—just as another one sprouted from the ground and launched another attack. He kicked out and thrashed at the mushroom with his blade. But the more he cut and slashed, the more mushrooms appeared from the darkness to replace the first attackers.

They were outnumbered ten to one.

Kara's head started to throb again just as a massive killer-mushroom charged towards her with a mouth full of gnashing teeth. It was going to crush her like a tomato.

CHAPTER 10

AMBUSHED

KARA FLATTENED HERSELF ON the ground just as the mushroom's body passed over her head.

Whoosh!

Her bangs lifted off her forehead in its wind, and a bit of earth spattered on her face. She rolled over and jumped to her feet brandishing her sword.

Her friends were already in combat.

Jenny kicked at a large mustard-yellow mushroom creature and leapt over it just as it tried to wrap its limbs around her ankle.

"It's an ambush! What kind of magic is this?" she screamed as she hit the mushroom with her bow and it snapped back with an angry mouth.

"We should have packed frying pans instead of daggers," yelled David as he hacked away at a blue and white polka dot mushroom. "We could have stopped for lunch."

More mushroom creatures shot out from the darkness and surrounded Peter. He jumped back in surprise and hit at the attacking beasts desperately with his moonstone.

"Kara!"

She heard David's scream before she saw that he was surrounded by a mass of swirling mushrooms. "Get out of here! Run back to the entrance and get out!"

Crazed mushrooms launched themselves from the shadows and attacked him from every side. He hacked away at their limbs with his soul blade, but the ground trembled and responded by sprouting more of its creatures. For every one David cut, ten more thrashed out at him. There were just too many.

But Kara wasn't about to give up—too much depended on her. She took courage from her friends and jumped into the fray with the violent mushroom beasts. She hacked and whacked with all her mortal strength. With every hit of her soul blade, her bones reverberated all the way to her chattering teeth. But she didn't give up. She screamed in rage as she cut, kicked, punched, and pulled at every giant vegetable that came near her friends.

"It's a trap!" cried David as he kicked back at a large purple maw that tried to puncture his abdomen. "The witches sent us to our deaths! They'll wish they'd been separated at birth when I get through with them."

"Then why don't you find us a way to escape, genius," said Kara breathlessly.

David jumped over the tangled mess of snapping chops. The moonstone's light bounced off the black cave walls as he ran. He was covered in black earth. He fought his way through the tangle of mushrooms and slipped into another passageway to the right side of the cave.

After a few seconds of silence, his voice rang out. "The cream-of-mushroom soup didn't follow me. It's clear! Come on guys—we can't fight these things—hurry!"

His moonstone's light wavered.

Kara waited for Peter and Jenny to make it through before she jumped over the mushroom militia and slipped into the network of underground tunnels. She landed softly next to Jenny and Peter who were dusting themselves off. They were a little shaken and covered in dirt, but otherwise they didn't look harmed.

David inspected the new tunnel. "Mushrooms belong on pizza—they don't normally grow arms and legs and want to eat us. First giant water fists, then man-eating mushrooms—what's next? Killer carrot sticks? Actually, that would be really funny."

He walked further down the passageway. The moonstone's light made his blue eyes sparkle.

"Don't get too comfortable," said Kara. "I have a feeling we haven't seen the worst of it yet."

Peter adjusted his glasses. "The Fay sisters warned us about the cave—about the evil that was in here. They said it wouldn't like the spirit walkers."

"I don't care what those stupid women said," said Jenny. "I hate them."

She flung her bow across her shoulders, and her face hardened. She looked at Kara questioningly. "Which way do we go now? There are more tunnels up to the right."

Kara strained through the darkness. "Look, there's light at the end of this tunnel. It could be a trap, but it could also lead us to the witch. I say we follow it. What do you—"

The rest of her words were lost as a sudden dark presence overcame her. It was a warning. She couldn't shake off the feeling of danger. Her friends were in danger—she was sure of it. Whatever was inside this cave—she knew it would be the demise of the guardians—she would have to make them leave and go on alone.

"Uh...guys, I think you should go back," said Kara.

She addressed her friends as calmly as she could. "I can feel something dangerous coming. The witches were right—this is suicide. Your souls are in danger in here."

"Never," David raised the tone of his voice. "I'm not abandoning you here in this freak show. It's not going to happen."

"David's right." Jenny squeezed Kara's arm gently. "We knew what we were doing when we took the assignment. We knew the dangers."

Kara shook her head. "But these dangers are not what we're used to. This magic this is different. We're not fighting against demons anymore. I should go in there alone. You can wait for me back at the entrance. I'm sure it'll be fine—"

"Forget it." David set his jaw. "You don't have a choice. We're coming with you and that's the end of it." He turned around but not before Kara saw the anger on his face. She felt a stab in her chest.

Jenny let go of her arm and smiled gently. "Like it or not, we're coming with you." Kara opened her mouth to protest, but closed it again. She knew it was no use to argue.

"Keep your eyes open for any more killer mushrooms."

David lifted the moonstone and lit the path in white light again. He looked up the side of the passageway and raised his arms.

"We come in peace," he said out loud. "Keep your broccoli and asparagus in their pots."

Kara sighed. "Come on then, we have a date with a witch."

They walked in silence. The cave looked identical everywhere. It was a labyrinth of underground tunnels. Water dripped and their treads echoed and were amplified by the cave until they sounded like the beating of drums.

Suddenly, the cave wall to their right was illuminated with spots of multicolored light. At first Kara thought they were minerals in the rock, but she soon realized that they were moving like glowing worms. They twisted and coiled around one another until they formed a series of symbols. Then they held themselves in position. They looked like words on a blackboard.

"Hang on," said Kara as she halted. "Look—do these look like words to you?" She edged closer for a better look.

"Don't get too close," said Jenny suspiciously, "it's probably another trap."

Kara's eyes widened. "I can read it...it says, '*Spirit walkers beware. Go back if you value your soul.*'"

"We already know that, *cave*." David held the moonstone closer to the worms. "Tell us something we don't know."

The glowworms shifted and rolled and another series of words appeared.

"*Beware of the witch,*" read Peter. "This is fascinating. The cave walls are actually communicating with us. Clearly, they've been bewitched or something."

"Really, you think?" said David sarcastically. "What—the killer fungi didn't give it away. I hadn't noticed them attacking us."

Kara watched him take a slow step back to keep more distance between him and the glowing worms.

Kara agreed that this was some sort of magic. And yet, she wasn't frightened by it. In fact, she felt drawn to it, curious as to how it all worked. The worms were cute, in a slimy way.

The letters shifted again and a new set of words appeared. "*Watch out for the big rocks, spirit walkers,*" read Kara.

She frowned and looked to the others. "What do you think that means? What rocks?" she searched the shadow covered path. "We're in a cave—there are rocks everywhere. Do you guys see any big rocks that stand out from the others?"

"Nope." David scanned the area with the moonstone. "The witch is toying with us. She's probably watching us right now and having a good laugh. Come on out, witch!"

Peter scratched his head. "It could be a clue..."

"I doubt that," said Jenny, "considering the cave's murderous intentions."

Kara turned back to the sign. "What do you mean by big rocks? Can you tell us where they are? We don't see any rocks?"

She stood waiting for a moment for the sign to change, but it didn't. When it finally did shift, the words faded, and the worms disappeared back into cracks in the wall as though the sign had never happened.

"So much for that," said Jenny.

Kara shrugged. "Come on, let's keep moving—"

BOOM!

The thick cave wall splintered in an explosion of dust and shards of rock. Two eight foot tall man-like creatures stepped out from the shadows. They were stocky and massive—if mountains could have offspring Kara decided they would be them. Their thick chests rose and fell with every breath, and instantly she knew they weren't demons—they were magic forces sent by the witch.

Their crusty gray hide looked like stone. Like great apes, they moved slowly, as if they were struggling to move their stone bodies. The tallest and widest of the creatures held a battle-axe in his massive hand. The other dragged a spiked club. Their yellow eyes glowed with supernatural intelligence.

"Uh...guys," said David. "Who called for reinforcements?"

In a great leap, the giants hurtled towards them.

CHAPTER 11

ATTACK OF THE ROCK-MEN

PETER TRIED TO TURN and run, but he wasn't fast enough. The battle-axe caught him on the side of his legs and tore them off completely. He flew in the air like a ragdoll and landed in a crumpled heap on the round. His mortal legs landed in a pile next to him. He opened his mouth in a soundless scream. His face was a mask of horror, and he cradled what was left of his legs with his arms.

Jenny nocked two arrows at once and let them go. They hit the second giant in the chest, but bounced off like tennis balls—they didn't even leave a mark. She nocked another three, let them go, and again they bounced off the creature with no effect. She staggered back in shock. The giant lunged at her and hit her in the chest with a great swing of his club. She flew into the air and crashed into the cave wall.

Kara could see Jenny's essence seeping out of the many deep holes in her body—as though she was wearing a polka dot outfit. She slumped to the ground and didn't move.

Without thinking, Kara charged at the giant that had attacked Jenny. She wasn't sure what she was going to do—she just wanted it dead, or at least hurt it. Her anger surged through her like a hot fever. She thought she could sense her elemental power awaken, like a light buried deep within her, slowly coming to life. She felt her confidence return—she would blast them to pieces with her power. She would save her friends...

But then the light flickered and died.

Kara staggered and nearly fell, the fear was so overwhelming, and for the first time on a mission, she felt vulnerable and weak. Without her elemental powers to fall back on, her mortal body was no match for the giant rock-men. She had nothing but a puny dagger—as useless as a toothpick against mountains of rock. She swallowed back the bile in her throat. What a fool she had been.

She looked up into the wicked yellow eyes and prepared herself. A giant club with spikes like razor sharp knives flashed towards her. She lifted her arm to protect her face—

Crack!

Pain shot up her arm. She flew back and tumbled to the ground. Her eyes watered as the excruciating pain emanated from her broken limb. Her cry died in her throat, and her arm hung lifelessly on her side, as though it were dead. Grinding her teeth, she felt the ruptures inside her arm. The shattered bones felt like shards of broken glass poking her skin. Wetness trickled down the side of her face. Her jacket sleeve was stained with red. The ground wavered, and she felt herself drifting into the darkness...

"Kara, get back!"

David rushed past her, determined to attack the two rock monsters.

He ducked as a giant battle-axe missed his head by an inch, displacing a few locks of his blond hair. He rolled and jumped back on his feet, swinging his blade. He barely dodged the great strikes, but he sidestepped and blocked them with all the strength his M-5 suit could muster.

The other monster charged again.

David raised his moonstone in an arc and let it go. The brilliant globe left a single trail of white light behind it as it lit up the cave and flew into the giant's face.

The moonstone exploded, and the rock giant disappeared behind a cloud of brilliant white light. For a moment, Kara thought David had destroyed the creature.

But when the mist evaporated the creature stood there, unscathed. Its ugly face was contorted in an angry frown. It let out a battle cry and charged at David, swinging its club.

"Oops, I think the big guy's angry—but it was worth a shot to see that look on his face. Did you two trolls ever hear of *moisturizers?*"

David jumped in the air as the club grazed the soles of his boots. He landed on the ground and rolled—again the giant spiked club missed him by inches. He pushed up, parried, and jammed his blade with all his strength into the creature's chest—

The blade bounced back. The giant wrapped his great hand around David's neck and lifted him up easily. David kicked out with his feet. His blade dropped to the ground. The giant roared, and green ooze splattered David's face. The rock-man sneered and squeezed harder. Kara saw the panic on David's face. The creature smiled, exposing rows of crooked teeth. David was going to get squeezed to death.

Kara ignored her panic. She searched the ground for her blade with her unbroken left hand and touched its cool metal. With trembling fingers, she clasped the handle as hard as she could and struggled onto her shaky legs. She waited until the dizziness passed and staggered forward towards David's attacker. She couldn't see the other monster, although she knew it was there somewhere. She could hear it breathing.

She heard Peter's moaning from behind her, but heard nothing from Jenny. Focusing all her strength on putting one foot in front of the other, she thought only of saving David. Blinking the wetness from her eyes, her right arm hanging loosely at her side, she pushed on. She couldn't just stand there and do nothing while her friends' souls were about to die. She knew she would die trying to save her friends. There was no way she could defeat the stone monsters, but she had to try.

The other rock monster marched towards her. It watched her every move, and its battle-axe glinted in the soft grey light. Kara cringed at the remnants of Peter's essence on the edge of the blade. It looked as though it had been dipped into a bucket of glowing white paint.

She measured them as best she could in the dim light. She knew their skin was unbreakable and as solid as rock. It was like fighting off giant cement boulders. And yet, these were living and breathing creatures, not demons. If demons had weaknesses, then these creatures must have a weak spots, too. Maybe they were like dragons whose underbellies were the weakest.

"Kara, run!" screamed David, as he dangled in the air, his face screwed up in pain. "Get out while you still can."

"No. I'm not leaving you."

Kara set her jaw and planted herself before the two giants. She was surrounded. Her heart thumped in her ears like a machine gun—she could hardly hear herself think. She searched the giants' skin, but she couldn't see any weak spots on them. Their skin all looked the same...except for a beige discoloration that marked both sides of their chests just below their armpits—perhaps weakness in their crusty hide.

It was her only chance.

The largest of the creatures stepped forward. With a wicked sneer he swung his battle-axe skillfully and towered easily over her.

With her last ounce of courage, and before the giant realized what she was planning, she leaped forward and jammed the blade into the creature's side.

The blade perforated the skin.

The giant threw back his head and howled. It thrashed its arms in the air and knocked Kara to the ground. It yanked the blade out of its side. Dark blood gushed from the wound. The giant staggered and fell on its knees.

If there was blood, then it could be killed. Kara pushed herself back onto her feet. A wave of renewed strength washed over her. She could save them all—but she needed another weapon.

As she searched the ground for David's blade, something hard hit her head. Stars exploded behind her eyes.

And then everything went black.

CHAPTER 12

OLGA THE CORNISH WITCH

KARA DREAMED SHE WAS hanging upside down like a piece of meat. Everything hurt, especially her throbbing head. Usually in dreams, you don't feel pain. Why did she feel pain?

It wasn't a dream.

She peeled open her crusted lashes and looked around. Blood gushed to her head, and she fought the urge to vomit. Pressure pushed at the back of her eyes, like they were just about to pop out of her head. She *was* hanging upside down. Her head hovered twelve inches off a moss-covered ground. As her eyes adjusted to her surroundings, she could tell she was in a clearing in a forest and not in the cave. A faint whisper of waves reached her, the ocean wasn't too far away.

The air smelled like a mixture of manure and chicken noodle soup. A large cauldron sat above a blazing fire in the middle of the clearing and right in front of Kara. Yellow vapors coiled from the rim and disappeared into the dark orange sky. A few skulls littered the ground around the cauldron. Because she was upside down, Kara couldn't tell if they were animal or human.

She twisted her head around. Orange light poured between the gaps in the trees. A great tree trunk was rooted in the middle of the clearing. Its top was cut, and a crooked wooden house sat above it, nestled between branches. The house had a moss-covered roof, and red light glowed from four round openings that Kara guessed were windows. It had a wraparound porch. Ropes dangled from a wooden platform, which was connected to a rectangular wood contraption with a door on the ground below. It was the strangest house Kara had ever seen. A house in a tree—it had to be Olga's house. Only a witch could live in a tree...or squirrels.

Looking around, she couldn't see any witch or any human form. Only crows nestled in the trees nearby, their yellow eyes fixed on Kara.

She tried to swallow, but her throat was raw. She was incredibly thirsty. As if on cue, her stomach growled loudly. She was starving, and she felt like she was about to become someone else's meal. She turned her head around and winced. Her right arm throbbed. It was pinned against her body awkwardly, making the pain worse. Her heart pounded, and her ribs ached. Sweat trickled down her back. She swallowed back her tears.

Moving her head slowly to her left she could make out three other hanging bodies, chained up like cocoons just like her. From what she could see, their M-suits were still intact—their angel souls were still alive. David's head was turned to the side, so she couldn't tell if he was conscious. But still, the situation was worse that she could have possibly imagined. This was not how she planned on meeting the witch, hanging from her feet like a bat. She felt the sickness rise in her throat again. She had to get out of these chains...

She struggled against her restraints, but it was useless. She couldn't break through metal chains with a broken arm. She was just a regular mortal.

"Kara..." whispered a voice. Kara turned her head to the left. David's blue eyes were staring right at her.

"David!" she whispered back. "Thank God, you're okay."

"I wouldn't call this okay, but yeah—I'm still in one piece. But I can't say the same about Peter. He's not looking good."

Kara looked past David and saw Jenny. Her wide green eyes looked her way, but Peter's eyes were closed. His skin was a transparent color, and he wasn't moving. Where his legs should have been, she could see short stumps with ends that emitted dim light. She had to get Peter back to Horizon before his soul died.

"We have to get him out of here." Kara bucked and kicked as hard as she could.

In her anger, she forgot her pain and cursed herself for being so foolish. How could she fight against giant rock men or metal chains? Had Ariel known about this? Had she sent Kara and her friends to their deaths?

Kara felt it was all her fault, and if they died she would never forgive herself.

She could not let her friends die. She closed her eyes and focused all her energy deep inside herself, in her soul, where her elemental power once belonged.

She felt something rise deep inside—there was something there—she could feel it. She focused all her strength on it. She called to it. It answered with a spark, then a warm ripple. It came to her—

"I'd stop doing that if you know what's good for you," said a voice.

The connection died, and Kara opened her eyes.

A short and skeletal woman stood before her. If Kara had not known better, she would have thought her a ghost. Her long yellow toenails peeked from under a layer of shredded lace. A dilapidated gray wedding gown encrusted with dirt and grime hung loosely on her skinny frame. Wisps of white hair peppered her nearly bald head and made her unnaturally large ears stick out even more. Her olive colored skin hung loosely around her face in many layers. She looked ancient—her back was hunched over, and she leaned on a walking stick that looked like an old tree branch. She wore a small leather pouch tied to a belt around her waist. One glowing yellow eye focused on Kara. Where the other should have been, there was only a blackened hollow hole.

But her one glowing yellow eye was alert and full of vigor.

Kara averted her eyes from the hollow eye socket. "I wasn't doing anything—"

"Oh, yes you were, girlie," rasped the woman, in a voice that sounded like Fay sisters' voices. The old woman wobbled closer to Kara. Her bony knees cracked as she came forward.

Kara opened her mouth to say, *no I wasn't,* but decided to drop it.

"Are you...are you Olga?" she asked instead, in the most polite voice she could muster hanging upside down.

The woman ignored Kara as she inspected her closer. Kara could smell her sour breath. The dirty lace dress tickled her face.

The woman stepped back after a moment. Then she reached up to her face with a *pop*—pulled out her yellow glowing eye.

"What the—" said David, as he stifled a laugh.

The old woman bent over Kara with her eye in her hand and moved it along her body like a magnifying glass, stopping every now and then. "Hmm...oh, yes, yes, yes," she mumbled while dragging her yellow eye over Kara.

"I told you she had it, Henry. It's as plain as rain. I see it—it's all over her."

Kara blinked. The yellow eye stared at her. The black pupil moved around inside the glowing yellow ball. Kara opened her mouth to scream, but the woman moved her eye away and was now inspecting Kara's feet.

Kara shared a look with David. Despite the fact that they were hanging upside down, he was smiling. Jenny looked disgusted.

Finally, after a few minutes inspecting Kara with her eye, the old woman popped her eye back in its socket and twisted it back into place as if it were a bolt.

The old woman leaned on her stick with both hands.

"See Henry? I told you she had it. Haven't seen one with so much of it for a very long time, I must say. How very interesting."

Kara turned her head, but she couldn't see the one she called Henry anywhere. Maybe the old woman was senile.

"Uh...excuse me, but are you Olga?"

The old woman didn't answer so Kara continued. "My friends and I are looking for her. We were told we'd find her somewhere near the cave. It's very important that I speak with her."

"These *spirit walkers*," the old woman spat, "are not your friends, girlie. You should stay away from them. Spirits should stay dead—away from the world of the living. It is against the laws of nature."

She hit her stick against the earth, and the ground trembled at its touch like a mini earthquake.

"Listen, lady." said David. "It's not like we wanted to come here and ruin your tea party, but we didn't have a choice. Could you just answer her so we can get out of here—"

"Silence! Do not speak to me, spirit walker!" The old woman's dress billowed around her in a gust of wind. "Dare speak to me again, and I will destroy you like I destroyed the others of your kind—"

"Mommy, can I do it please?" whined a voice. And for the first time Kara noticed that the rock giants were sitting comfortably in the shadows, looking bored. "Bill crushed the last spirit walkers—and he didn't even leave me one—it's not fair," moaned the smaller rock giant.

The rock giant, Bill, smashed the other giant on the head with his battle-axe. "You're such a baby, Will. It's not my fault I'm a better fighter than you. Mom always said *I* was the strongest—"

"Yeah...but you're ugly."

BOOM!

142

Will hit Bill in the chest with a powerful blow of his club, and Bill went crashing down. Dust and pebbles flew in the air as the two giants attacked each other.

"Boys, enough!" The old woman slammed her walking stick on the ground. Two electric tendrils shot out from it and coiled around the giants. With a zap, the current separated them and blasted them apart.

Smoke rose from their bodies as they rubbed their heads. They stared across at each other angrily, but didn't go at it again.

"He started it," said Will with a pout.

"No I didn't, you did," said Bill angrily.

Will jumped to his feet. "You did!"

"Stop this nonsense at once!" cried the old woman. "Don't make me boil you for soup."

She lifted a bony finger at them. "You know what happened last time."

Will slumped to the ground and folded his arms around his chest. Kara thought she saw a grin on Bill's crusty face.

The old woman turned her attention back to Kara. "Didn't know what I was thinking, when I adopted these rock trolls—should have left them in the woods to rot!"

She raised her voice. "And don't you dare tell me I told you so, Henry, I'm not in the mood today."

Pain shot through Kara's arm. Tears rolled down her forehead and onto the ground below. "Please Olga—I know you're the witch—we need your help."

"My help? And why should I help you, girlie?"

"Because you're the only one who can help—" Kara faltered and winced. "—who can help us? Please...my arm," Kara cringed. "It's broken. I need to sit down—"

The witch snapped her fingers, and Kara fell to the ground headfirst. She lifted her head—the chains had vanished. Hot pain exploded in her arm as she struggled to her feet. She did her best not to cry out. The ground wavered, and she steadied herself. Something was missing—her backpack. She must have dropped it in the cave. She licked her dry lips—she was so thirsty.

"Here, drink this." A wooden cup appeared in Olga's hand.

Kara took the cup in her shaking fingers. Steam rose from the rim, and the sweet aroma of tea rose in her nose. She brought the cup to her trembling lips and gulped it down in two swallows. Warmth spread through her body immediately. Only then did she think that it might be poison, but it was too late. She stared at the bottom of the empty cup. It was the best tea she had ever tasted.

"Don't worry, it's not poison," said Olga, as though reading her thoughts.

Kara stared at her hands. The cup had vanished. She looked up into Olga's yellow eye. The old witch was smiling as though she was amused to see Kara so bewildered. Kara's arm started to hurt again, and she cradled it with her other arm.

"Don't move," ordered Olga, and she hit the ground twice with her staff.

"What—?"

The ground shifted and moaned beneath Kara's feet. The earth broke and soil spat out from deep gashes like mini volcanoes. Then roots sprouted from the ground near her feet. They rose and coiled around her like thick lassoes, until she was covered completely, mummified by roots. They went up through her coat, touched her skin, and coiled around her broken limb. A warm pulsing enveloped her. The rough roots squeezed her gently, but she wasn't afraid. It was like she had been wrapped in a warm leather blanket. She was embraced in the warm comfort from the roots. She could already sense its healing powers, like warm sunrays.

And then all at once, the roots slithered off Kara and disappeared back into the ground like giant worms.

Kara lifted her right arm and inspected it. There was no more pain. She flexed her arm muscles—they were as good as new, maybe even better.

"That's amazing? How did they do that?"

Olga grinned. "Our mother Earth has many healing powers." Olga turned around and spoke to no one in particular. "Of course, I know. You'd better be quiet, Henry, or I'll throw you in the cauldron again!"

Kara searched behind Olga. "Who are you talking to?"

Olga pointed to a human skull resting on a wooden stool near the cauldron—Henry.

"To Henry, husband number thirteen—doesn't even know when to shut up, even in death."

Kara eyed Henry nervously.

"I hate to interrupt your lovely bonding, but...a little help here?" David twisted against his restraints. "I'm going to lose it if I don't get out of this soon."

Olga snapped her fingers, and a metal chain twisted around David's mouth, silencing him. He frowned and yelled angrily through his metal muzzle.

Kara lifted her hands in surrender. "Please, Olga. These are my friends. They mean you no harm, I promise. They came here with me to find you."

The old witch shook her head. "Spirit walkers are sworn enemies of our kind. They are not your friends, girlie."

Kara planted her feet. "My name is Kara. I'm on an important mission for the legion of angels. And these angels here are my friends. Please let them go. They are hurt and might die if I can't get them back to Horizon—"

Olga lifted her hand. "I'm not interested in the dealings of spirit walkers. The dead should stay *dead*. They shouldn't be roaming the earth in these corrupted body bags. It goes against the laws of nature. Spirits should stay in the land of the spirits and not mingle in the land of the living."

Kara could sense that it wasn't going to be easy to pursue her for help, if she felt so strongly about the angels. Kara was angry with Ariel. Ariel knew that the witch had already killed some guardians—and she had still sent them here anyway. She wouldn't forgive her for that.

"There's a Dark warlock that's killing people," Kara blurted before she knew what she was doing. "He's collecting souls—he's infected thousands already. If we don't stop him, they're all going to die, including my mom. Please—I beg you, help us."

The witch measured Kara for a moment then closed her single eye. She stood for a moment without moving and then said, "Go. Fetch the pendant next to Henry. Don't worry, he can't bite anymore, I saw to that."

"Mom, I'll go get it for you," said Bill. He grinned at Will, and his yellow eyes glowed with mischief.

Will jumped to his feet, and Kara felt a small tremor beneath her boots. "Not fair! I want to go get it!"

"Both of you shut up!" yelled Olga. "You can't touch it with your big stupid fingers—you'll crush it into dust, and then where would we be, eh? Now sit and be quiet!"

The ground shook as Will fell back down. Both rock giants glared at each other.

Kara looked back at David who raised his eyebrows in a way that said, *go get it*.

Kara could see that Jenny's attention was focused on Peter, and if angels could cry, she was sure she'd be balling her eyes out.

Olga still had her eyes closed when Kara ventured towards Henry. She passed the cauldron and stole a look inside. Carrot and potato cubes bobbed in a thick creamy mixture. It looked like a giant vegetable soup, bubbling happily. It smelled wonderful, and her stomach growled. It took a lot of effort not to dunk her head in there and swallow a mouthful. Will and Bill were staring at her as they polished their weapons. It was clear they wanted to use her as target practice.

Leaving the soup behind, Kara had a good view of Olga's little wooden cottage nestled on the top of a great pine tree. Massive branches held it up, like a hand clutching an ashtray. It was even more crooked up close. Wood planks and beams jumbled together in a big puzzled mess. It was a miracle it didn't fall apart in a gust of wind. There were no visible stairs to go up. Maybe the witch floated to the front door? A large hand-painted sign at the top read: "An Old Bat A Witch & 3 Monsters Live Here."

Kara wasn't sure whether to laugh or take the sign seriously. Maybe there were three monsters after all—this was a witch's house.

Without further hesitation, Kara walked around the other side of the cauldron. Henry the skull sat comfortably on a plush cushion made of red and gold silk atop a small wood bench. It could have been his seat once upon a time, before he became a human cranium. He looked like a normal skull, except for the fact that his mouth was clamped shut with rusted nails. Kara wondered if he had acquired them before or after he became just a skull.

The pendant was wrapped around Henry like a large necklace.

She took a breath and grabbed the pendant. At first, she thought it might burn her or turn her into a bug or something. But nothing happened. She held it up in her hand. Runes were etched into a stone the size of her palm that hung from a black leather cord. The leather was cracked and worn, but the pendant glimmered without a scratch. Why did Olga need this?

Kara marched up to the witch and held out her hand. "Here," she said, "I did what you asked—now will you let my friends go?"

Olga examined the pendant, and then she pointed a skeletal finger at Kara. "You need to put that over your head, girlie. It'll protect you against evil."

Kara had no idea what she was talking about, but she lowered the pendant around her neck anyway. She looked over to Peter. His M-5 suit's skin was barely keeping his essence in. He was leaking out.

"Please, you must release my friends—they're going to die. I promise you, they're not the enemy."

The witch frowned and shook her head. "They were warned not to enter the cave. All spirit walkers who dare to enter my cave suffer the consequences. I will use their spirits for my spells. They are the most powerful, you know. But not to worry, girlie—they will be put to good use."

Kara approached Olga.

"But you don't understand. We've been sent here on a mission by the legion—all four of us. These spirit walkers are my friends, and we're here to save the mortals from the dark warlock. We were sent here to ask for your help. My boss told me that years ago the witches and angels fought together to rid the world of the dark warlocks. I'm asking for that allegiance once more."

Kara searched the old woman's face. "Please, Olga. Come with us and help us fight this evil before it's too late. You must help us."

For a moment Olga didn't move or say anything. Then, she snapped her fingers. David, Jenny and Peter fell to the ground, and their chains vanished.

Immediately, Jenny rushed over and cradled Peter in her arms. She rocked him gently and whispered in his ear. Kara felt a lump in her throat.

David pushed himself up on his feet and then steadied himself. "Took you long enough. Man, am I still upside down or are you upside down?" He rubbed his head.

Olga shuffled forward. She pulled out her eye and moved it slowly around David.

"Hmm. I see many ruthless spirits in you, spirit walker," she said and then wacked him with her staff.

"Ouch! What did you do that for?" he said and jumped away looking disgusted. "Can you put that eye back in its socket. It's freaking me out, grandma."

"Kara," said Jenny urgently. "We need to get Peter out of here. I think...I think he's dying."

Peter's M-suit was as thin as tissue paper, barely holding his essence.

Kara turned towards the old witch. "Please Olga," she pleaded. "We need your help to defeat the warlock. I'll do anything you want. Will you not help us?"

Olga twisted her eye back into its socket with a sickening *pop*. "I've already given you what I can. You already posses the skills that you need."

"Now you're talking crazy, grandma," said David. He and Kara shared a look.

Kara suppressed the panic in her voice when she spoke next. "We need magic to defeat the warlock. We don't have magic. You have the magic we need. Without you—we can't defeat him."

"Listen, madam witch, you're the only witch left to help us," said David. "Let's face it, you hate me and my friends," he lifted his fingers in a quote sign, "*spirit walkers*—we get that, but what Kara is trying to tell you is that your magic is the only thing that can save the mortals. You're the only one. If you don't help us—we're all doomed."

Olga watched them in silence and then shook her head. "But you are wrong—there is another who possesses the magic."

"Really," said David, raising his eyebrows. "Well now, your royal witchness, who is this person? Will they be as delightful as you?"

The old witch raised her hand and pointed to Kara.

"Her."

CHAPTER 13

FIRE RAIN

DAVID TWIRLED HIS FINGER next to his head and mouthed, *crazy*.

This was a disaster. Kara rubbed her temples. She could feel a major migraine coming.

"Olga, I don't have any magic skills—I can't even do a decent card trick. I'm just a normal teenage girl, with nothing special— except maybe that I'm on duty with the guardian angel legion. But I swear to you—I don't know anything about magic."

"You're elemental," said the witch. Her yellow eye twitched as she watched Kara intensely.

Kara's blood froze. She forced her lips to move. "What did you say?"

The witch smiled, and Kara noticed she only had one decayed front tooth.

"You're an elemental. I can see it plainly. Shut up, Henry, it's my time to speak. It's all over you, girlie. I've never met one with so much of it—how curious..."

Kara frowned. The Fay sisters had said something of the sort, too.

"I don't know what you mean by *elemental*. I know that I have elemental essence in me. It's what sets me apart from the other guardian angels—why most of them hate me, really. But I don't have any special powers as a mortal."

Olga stabbed her in the chest with her staff.

"But you do, girlie. You just don't know it."

David folded his arms over his chest. "Am I the only one who's confused here? Are you sure you're cooking soup in that thing? What's the witch talking about, Kara? Does this make sense to you?"

Kara met David's confused expression, but she couldn't answer him. It *was* making sense to her.

Olga ignored David and spoke only to Kara. "You know I speak the truth. You felt it before; when you were hanging from the chains—you were trying to summon it. It is why Shadow Cave opened up to you and let you pass—and why it let the spirit walkers pass without destroying them."

Kara shook her head even though she felt part of what Olga was saying was true. "You're wrong, Olga. I don't have any magic. I don't know any spells, I can't possibly be a witch."

"You're not a witch, girlie," laughed Olga. Wisps of thin hair swayed on the top of her balding head.

"You're an elemental. And elementals have a different kind of magic, a natural magic—a magic that comes from the earth. It has nothing to do with incantations and spells. It is nature's *energy*. It is the flow of mother earth's *power*."

David whistled loudly. "Whoa—that sounds wicked. I'd love to get some of that. I never thought witches could be so hot."

He smiled mischievously at Kara. "Can you curse me, sweet lady?"

Kara shot him a dirty look, and he pretended to seal his lips with his fingers.

Olga poked her in the stomach again, hard.

"Listen girlie, you *are* elemental. Nature's strength lies within you. You have the power to manipulate the energies, to summon mother earth's power."

The witch leaned on her staff, her yellow eye fixed on Kara. "You have the ability to feel and control these energies. Elementals are very rare and extremely powerful. You've admitted to having this power as a spirit walker—"

"Yes, but, it's not the same—"

"It is the same!" Olga raised her voice and hit Kara in the chest once again with her staff. "You are as elemental in spirit as you are in life. That doesn't change. You cannot change what you are—and that is, an *elemental*, a unique child of our mother earth."

Kara's head was spinning—an elemental in life as in death. Somehow, she believed the witch. It made sense. The energy she sensed as an angel was also in her mortal body, dormant and waiting to be awakened. Could it really be true? Suddenly, she didn't feel so weak anymore. Her elemental power was still in her—she just had to figure out how to tap into it.

154

She looked down at the pendant and took it in her hand. It was cool and light. "Then...I take it you're not coming with us. Am I right?"

Olga leaned on her staff again, as though it took all of her energy just to speak.

"If I leave these parts, I will die. I've only lived so long because the woods and the caves have protected me all these years. These wretched bones of mine would disintegrate if I stepped out. Even if I wanted to help you, I couldn't."

She bent closer to Kara. Her yellow eye twitched. "The Dark warlock is an evil creature, and if what you tell me is true, and he has risen from the dead, then you have a difficult and dangerous enemy on your hands. He will summon devilish powers from the darkness of the dead. His magic will be great and his servants plentiful. He knows I am a threat. Soon he will be coming for me—and you—you must leave now, girlie."

She pushed Kara with her staff. "He doesn't know about you—and it's best that we keep it that way until the time is right. Off you go..."

Kara knocked the staff away with her hand.

"But will you be safe? Can you protect yourself from him if he comes for you?"

She felt a sudden sadness for Olga and a need to protect her. She reminded Kara of her grandmother. She was old and frail. Kara didn't want anything bad to happen to her, even if she had almost killed her friends. The old witch was starting to grow on her, even Henry.

Olga ignored the question and pointed to the pendant.

"This is a witch's rune pendant of protection and elemental power. The pendant will energize and empower the magical intentions of their wearer. Earth, air, fire, water—the key to elemental power—these symbols are the mark of an elemental. The pendant will help you draw your powers and protect you against the Dark warlock."

"But how do I draw and use these powers?

The earth shook under Kara's feet.

A ball of liquid green fire fell from the sky and exploded in the clearing, setting the ground and trees ablaze. An earsplitting screech came from the trees, as though they were screaming in pain. Kara's chest tightened. She could almost feel their suffering as they burned. The green flames snaked up the trees and cast an eerie emerald glow on the clearing.

Bill and Will jumped up and brandished their weapons, a wild look in their yellow eyes.

"He has found me," said Olga, her gown flapped in a gust of wind as a yellow aura radiated from her skin. She turned to Kara. "There's no time. Listen to me and do exactly as I say."

Kara nodded and did her best to focus on Olga's face and not the green fire that threatened to burn her.

"You must destroy the Dark warlock *only* on the winter solstice—when the light half of the year is being turned over to the dark half. He will use the power of the souls he's collected already to raise *other* dark warlocks and devils. This is what he's been planning all along—to bring back the brethren. If he succeeds, he will bend the mortal world to his will. You must stop him. You cannot allow the solstice ritual to happen!"

The trees moaned, and Kara shivered. She couldn't move.

"But how do I do that? How do I stop him?" she yelled over the roar of the flames. "I don't know where the ritual will be!"

"He will be at the exact same place where he and his followers were destroyed a hundred and fifty years ago—look for Cleopatra's Needle, there you will find the entrance to the Warlock's lair."

"I have to go to Egypt?"

Olga's staff emitted a yellow color until it was completely covered. Even for an old witch, she looked dangerous and powerful. "New York city."

Kara just stared at her. "You're joking, right?"

The old witch ignored her.

"Search the tunnels beneath the great city. You need to seek out the old fool, Gideon. He's the only one who can help you now—you must do as he says. Understand?"

"But New York City is enormous. How can I find one old man?"

Olga's gaze went past Kara to the woods beyond. "Go to the tunnels. The pendant will guide you. Let the power flow naturally— it'll come to you."

"What? Seriously?" Kara stared at the green fire snaking its way towards her feet. "What kind of an answer is that? Olga, you need to give me more to go on—"

"You must get out of here, quickly!" said Olga.

The heat of the flames burned Kara's face. The smoke stung her eyes.

"But what about you? Are you going to be okay?" she said in between coughs.

Another ball of liquid fire crashed into the clearing. But this time it crashed into Olga's cottage. Within seconds the small cottage was enveloped in green flames. The rock trolls ran out and stood protectively around their mother.

Olga grabbed her staff with both hands. "I'll be fine—you must get out of here. This is warlock fire. The flames will kill you and your spirit walkers. If you value their lives, then get them out of here. I can take care of myself. Go back through the cave. Quickly, go now!"

"But—"

A great ball of green fire exploded at the base of Olga's cauldron. But instead of a blazing fire, a dozen frog-like creatures the size of adult bears sprouted from the flames. Their eyes glowed red, and a loud rumbling noise echoed in their throats. Gleaming symbols and runes covered their dark green slimy skin.

The rock trolls wielded their weapons and charged.

One of the creatures opened its maw. It was filled with rows of shark teeth, and it spat a green substance that hit Will in the chest and face.

He screamed in agony as a cloud of vapors coiled around his body. The green substance ate at his rock hide like some sort of acid, leaving holes and exposing his insides. Blood dripped from his charred face and chest. He fell to his knees, his eyes rolled back in his head, and he keeled over.

Bill screamed madly and ran into the wall of frog-creatures. He sliced the creature that killed his brother in half with one giant stroke of his battle-axe. As he turned, two more creatures leaped at him, and again he hacked them in half with his axe.

Dark blood splattered his face. Like a madman, he thrashed and slashed at the creatures, avenging his brother. But there were too many—the creatures attacked again, and Bill disappeared under a tangle of green limbs. She heard him scream and that was the last she saw of him.

More balls of liquid fire burst on the ground around Kara. More evil frog-like creatures sprouted from the flames, their red eyes searching for their next kill. They saw Kara and her friends, and in a great leap they soared through the air towards them—

A blast of yellow light hit the creatures in their chests, and they exploded into a cloud of green dust. The particles floated in the air and settled to the ground like falling ash.

Olga held her staff high above her head.

"Is that all you've got, warlock?" She called out into the green flames around her.

She hit her staff on the ground. Yellow whirlwinds thrashed forward and extinguished the green fires. "You warlocks are all the same. Always letting the help fight your battles. Show yourself, you coward!"

Another pulse of yellow energy flashed from Olga's staff and blasted more of the frog-creatures into piles of dust. Olga started to chant. Her single eye blazed in yellow, as though there was a fire inside.

"Kara, we have to get out of here." David grabbed Kara's arm and pulled her towards him. "I don't feel like getting eaten by giant frogs, and Peter's in no condition to fight. And I seriously doubt we can fight these things—we have to get back to Horizon. Now."

Peter lay crumpled in Jenny's arms, his essence nearly drained out of him. He looked dead already.

Kara saw the terror in Jenny's face.

She turned to David, "You're right, let's get out of here. Grab Peter and we'll make a run for it. Jenny, can you run?"

Jenny helped Peter onto David's back. Her angel essence glowed through the many gashes on her chest and face. "Yeah, I can run, but not for long. My M-suit's on its last legs."

With Peter secured on David's back, Kara ran from the clearing and headed towards the last of the forest that wasn't engulfed in flames. She stood in front of a wall of black trees. Where was the cave? She couldn't see past the branches. The woods were thick and impenetrable—it would take hours just to get through a few feet. She could hear the battle behind her. She started to panic.

"How do we get back to the cave?" Jenny settled beside her. Her green eyes were dull, and Kara could see the fear.

Kara cursed as she paced around the thick wall of trees. Where was the stupid cave?

The branches suddenly parted, and a tunnel appeared amongst the trees. And beyond the opening of twisted branches and roots stood a cleft in the side of the cliff—another entrance to the cave.

"Come on!" David ran through the opening and down the path. Jenny held her stomach and took off after him.

Kara started forward—a scream filled the night air.

A cold chill rolled down Kara's back. It was Olga. Kara whirled around.

A tall man draped in a black cloak stood in the middle of the clearing. Green circular symbols and runes glowed on his cloak and moved and shifted like liquid. His head was covered in a black hood—his face hidden in shadow.

Olga dangled by the throat from his glowing green fist—struggling and choking in his grasp. The warlock lifted Olga into the air and slammed his right fist into her abdomen.

Kara choked a scream as she watched the old woman fall to the ground and explode into a cloud of yellow dust. Kara stifled a sob.

The dark warlock turned his head slowly towards the edge of the forest where Kara stood. His glowing red eyes settled on her. She couldn't see his face—she couldn't even tell if he was human.

He lifted his arm and pointed a long gray finger at her—

Kara was thrown back with a powerful force. She landed hard on the ground. Her legs and arms were pinned together by a glowing green metal chain. Desperately, she rolled over and lifted her head. The warlock was walking towards her.

She screamed and fought against her chains, but it was like trying to peel open a giant's fist. It was pointless.

A green mist rose from the metal. She suddenly felt dizzy and very tired—she should rest. The ground was nice and soft and smelled like dandelions, a little rest wouldn't hurt anyone...

Kara...Kara...wake up!

Was that Olga's voice? Was she dreaming? Where was she?

She blinked away the spots from her vision. She knew something wasn't right. She strained to fight her sleepiness and recover long enough to think.

She had to get the chains off. She knew they were magical. Fight magic with magic—Olga had said her elemental power was still within her.

She concentrated on the feeling she had felt before. She searched deep inside herself for that light, that energy she had used when she was an angel. She let her emotions flow. Her anger about Olga's death washed through her as she concentrated.

The Warlock was only a few paces away—if she didn't do something now—she would be as good as dead.

Her heart raced. Every breath of air felt like vaporized acid. She choked through the green mist. She wasn't ready to die, not like this and especially not at the hands of some schizo-warlock man.

A flicker came from deep inside her, like a candle flame sputtering before it lights. The pendant burned against her chest, its own power vibrated against her skin. She looked down. The runes on the pendant glowed yellow like the morning sun and intensified. She relaxed and closed her eyes. She reached deep within herself, searching for that fountain of energy that was the source of her elemental power. Her mind touched an elemental black quiet, and a

162

cool rush of energy gushed up through her veins. It was different from the warm gush she had summoned when she was an angel—it was cool and smelled like spring. And just like that, she knew what to do.

The gust of power surged through her like a cool wind, overwhelming her senses with the smell of the earth. Like the feel of the wind on her face for the first time in her life, it exploded all at once, and she surrendered to it.

Silver sparks of energy danced on her skin. The earth around her rippled. Small white roots sprouted from the soil and snaked onto the poisonous green chains that held her captive. With a pop, the chains melted away as if they had been made of ice.

Kara jumped to her feet. The warlock froze, clearly not expecting Kara to free herself so suddenly. She didn't have time to think about what had just happened. And not waiting for him to try anything else, she turned and ran into the cave.

CHAPTER 14

NYC SUBWAY STATION

THE STREETS OF NEW YORK CITY were just as Kara remembered. Giant stone and glass buildings surrounded her on either side. Masses of people milled in and out of shops as they went about their daily routines. She had been here once before, in search of the missing field agent, Catherine, when she had first joined the CDD team. Only this time, she was alone.

She had left her friends at the foot of the cliff and had watched them disappear into the icy ocean. She hoped the Healing-Xpress would heal them. David had squeezed her hand gently and tried to convince her that this wasn't her fault. But she couldn't shake the feeling that she should have gone into the cave alone. If Peter's soul didn't recover, his true death would be on her.

The only good thing was that she had found her backpack in the middle of one of the passageways in the cave, as if it had been waiting for her. Maybe Olga's magic had kept it safe for her.

As Kara stood on the corner of 59th Street and Lexington Avenue, she wondered if Ariel and the legion had known that the old witch couldn't leave Shadow Cave? Had Ariel known that Kara's elemental powers might resurface in her mortal body— enough to take on the warlock?

But first she needed to find the man called Gideon. She figured the tunnels under the city had to be the subway system. But once she got there, she had no clue what to do. The New York subway system was gigantic...and time was running out.

She had waited ten hours for a flight. Today was December twenty first. Jetlagged and sore, Kara had only a few hours to find Cleopatra's Needle and destroy the dark warlock—all before the winter solstice. No pressure. Piece of cake. Just thinking about it made her feel sick. She clasped the pendant in her hand. How was she going to do it?

Kara followed the line of people milling down the 59th Street subway entrance. After studying the subway map, she saw that the N train would take her to 42nd street—but how would she find Gideon? Which tunnel would he be in? She didn't have time to ride the entire New York subway system.

Kara made her way along the concrete floors peppered with gum stains. She caught the appalling scent of cigarette smoke and bleach. The only source of light came from the long neon light fixtures that ran the length of the station. They flicked and buzzed as she passed under them. Except for some graffiti near the entrance, beige bricks covered the walls. She followed the signs for Downtown and Brooklyn.

She glanced at her watch—12:35 pm.

Crowds of people poured in through the other entrances.

And then she saw it—glowing green runes covered most of their faces. Just like her mother's and Sabrina's, their skin was a pasty grey color, and their eyes were sad and lifeless. Like robots, they shuffled through the crowds, not knowing that they had been marked by a dark warlock. They would soon be very sick and die—they would lose their souls.

She tightened her fists and rushed through the crowds. She was running out of time.

"Gideon, where are you?" she whispered.

The pendant brushed against her skin. She stopped and pulled it out. She traced her fingers over the symbols. The stone felt warm in her hand, and she could feel a rhythmic pulse almost like a vibration. The runes glowed yellow and the pendant rose from her hand and floated in the air like a tethered balloon. With the string taut, it pulled her westward, steering her like a floating compass.

She caught it in her hand and pulled it down, but the pendant rose again just like a bar of floating soap in a tub.

"Do you know where Gideon is?" she asked the pendant, feeling a little foolish. But she sensed it knew where he was.

The string pulled her westwards again. Kara let the pendant steer her. She hid it between her hands to avoid the weird stares she was getting from the passersby.

The pendant pulled her toward the sign for the N train, to Downtown and Brooklyn.

Suddenly, one after the other, the neon lights overhead began to explode. Kara and dozens more people were showered in shards of glass. She ran and cowered against the opposite wall, shaking tiny shards from her hair. People screamed as they ran for cover.

And then all the lights went out.

Kara and the others were left in complete darkness. Was it her power or the pendant's causing this? Then just before people started to panic, the lights flicked back on.

Kara prayed the lights would stay on. With the pendant still steering her, she took a deep breath and walked towards the ticket booth. The lights flickered above her, but stayed on. She sidestepped and swerved in and around the crowds, trying to avoid them as best she could as the pendant pulled her along.

Kara reached the ticket booth just in time to remember that she didn't have any money.

She doubled back. People poured through the turnstiles. She watched them for a moment and then flung herself between a bald man in a large grey trench coat and a heavy middle-aged woman with more bags than she could carry. She slipped through the turnstile easily.

But just not fast enough.

"HEY, YOU," yelled the ticket master through his glass cage. "You need to pay. I'm calling the police."

He pounded his fists against the glass. "Get back here!"

Kara tightened the straps on her backpack and made a run for it. She rocketed down the stairs to the first platform. She stole a look behind—no one was chasing her. She relaxed a little and looked around. Besides the nasty garbage and pee smell, the subway looked normal. It was huge, with three concrete platforms separated by subway tracks.

Masses of people stood waiting for their trains and more than half glowed with green warlock runes. No one took any notice of her. She appeared to be the only person who could see the warlock's mark. It pained her to watch them.

The pendant pulled her to the left of the platform. Kara obeyed the amulet and followed its direction. She reached the end of the platform, where the tunnel began, and still the pendant pulled. It wanted her to go into the subway tunnel. She remembered reading about people living under the subway system, in old abandoned tunnels. Maybe Gideon was one of those people? Kara held onto the sidewall and peeked into the depths of the tunnel. It curved and then disappeared into shadow. Wind brushed against her cheek. The platform vibrated slightly. Kara turned and saw a small bright light at the opposite end of the tunnel. It was getting larger by the second. She didn't want to slip and fall into the train's path accidently. She didn't have time to jump down now and stepped back from the edge. The oncoming train squealed as it rushed past her and then came to a halt. Her clothes fluttered in the strong gust of wind.

"THERE SHE IS! GET HER!"

Kara whirled around. Three men in uniform with walkie-talkies sprinted towards her pointing, their faces contorted angrily.

She turned her back to them, whistling causally and at the last movement jumped into the waiting train. The doors slid shut. The train kicked into life. The men in uniforms hit the glass with their fists, but they were too late. Kara watched their angry faces disappear in a blur as the train pulled away from the platform. Sighing loudly she threw herself into an empty seat. Now what?

As if in response, her head started to throb again, the pain was worsening by the hour. And to make matters worse, she felt weaker, like the first signs of a cold. Pressing her nose against the glass, she strained to see through the dark tunnels. No sign of an old man anywhere. This was crazy. She would have to get off at the next stop and slip onto the tracks to look for him. It was the only way.

The train car was alive with people young and old. The dark warlock's glowing green runes were everywhere. A sudden feeling of evil came at her again, only this time it was stronger, as though the threat were closer. The pulsing increased on the pendant. It hovered for a moment, and then it dropped back down against her chest.

The lights went out.

The train stopped with a powerful jerk, as if it had hit a brick wall. People and their belongings went crashing to the ground. Kara grabbed the metal pole just as the train finally lurched to a stop. People screamed. The emergency lights flicked on, bathing everyone in a blood-red color.

Kara's vision adjusted to the semi-darkness, and she could make out other tunnels winding away into the darkness. They were somewhere buried deep in the underground train system. The cars in front of them were twisted and off the tracks in a big Z. Kara felt a gigantic bump beginning to rise on the side of her head. Had they hit something?

A middle-aged man started to curse loudly about missing an important meeting.

BOOM!

The metal roof of the car collapsed, as though a giant boulder had landed on it.

She pulled out her blade and waited.

The train shook as a series of thumps and crashes came from the roof, as though it was raining rocks. Kara covered her ears as an eerie piercing screech wailed over the frantic screams of the people inside the train. The train shook like a boat in a storm. Terrified people left their belongings behind and ran past Kara to the next car. As she rushed to join them—her body jerked back. Her coat was caught in the gap in the seats.

"This is *so* not happening right now." She was struggling to free her jacket when the back of the car was blasted open. She ducked as sharp metal planks flew past her head.

A rat the size of an English Mastiff crawled into the car. Its black fur glowed as green runes moved around on its body. Its glowing red eyes were fixed on her. It snarled, revealing four enormous incisors that belonged more on a saber tooth tiger than a rat. A thick black tail twitched behind it nervously.

It sat still for a moment and opened its large maw.

"I see we meet again, *elemental*." Its voice screeched like feedback on an old radio station, and Kara knew right away the rat was just a conduit for someone else.

Green ooze dripped from the corners of its jaw as it continued, "The witch thought she could hide you from me, but I have eyes and ears everywhere—and I know everything. You cannot escape."

The car swayed as five other enormous rats crawled through the broken windows. People from the next car screamed and shouted, but the new rats stayed behind the rat that had been speaking to Kara, as if waiting for orders.

Kara's pulse raced, and the pendant felt like she was wearing a brick. She waved her soul blade before her. "What do you want from me, *rat*?"

"Your little escape in the woods was remarkable," said the same rat. "I've been wondering about you—about what you are. You left me quite vexed, you see. You're not a *normal* teenager, are you? It takes great power to cut through my bonds—and then it occurred to me that you must be an elemental. The earth's energy responded to your call for help. I was very impressed. I could use someone like you in my circle—"

"Never," Kara spat. "You steal the souls of mortals and leave them for dead. You're a vile creature—and I'm going to stop you for good."

The rat's eyes widened as it laughed. "Yes, I thought you might say that."

The rat's nose twitched. "I'm afraid you pose too much of a threat for me to let you live. I would kill you myself, but I'm sure my little pets will finish the job for me."

"I'm not that easy to kill."

The rat sneered. "You're just a teenage girl with a little power, and I will kill you. I am far more powerful than you, elemental. You are alone—your spirit walker friends cannot help you now. I will tear you apart, and my pets will feast on your blood."

The rat leaped.

Kara reached over and cut her jacket free, just as a giant paw with razor sharp nails tore the seat in half. Blocking another swing, she jumped onto the next seat. She doubted her chances of survival against six giant magical rats, but she would avenge Olga's death, even if it meant dying in the process.

Whack!

A tail hit her from behind, and Kara fell hard on the metal floor. Hot pain exploded in her knee. She pushed herself up.

Suddenly she was being dragged backwards. She turned around. Blood seeped from her jeans where the rat's front claws had perforated her leg like five knives. It pulled her toward it. She looked into the mouth of the giant rat and putrid drool dripped onto her face. It lowered its head.

Kara brought her blade up from under the creature's jaw in an arc and pushed the blade into its brain. Green ooze splattered the floor. The rat dropped dead. The runes vanished from its fur. It sizzled and popped and slowly returned to its original size, the size of Kara's boot.

She heard nails scratching metal, and the five other rats charged.

Kara ran towards the exit door at the back of the train. She wrapped her hand on the handle and pulled, but it would not move.

She pulled and pulled. Nothing. A man's face watched her from the other side of the glass. He shook his head. And Kara understood—they had locked her in.

She banged on the door. "Please, let me out. You can't do this! Open the door!"

The man just shook his head. Another man came, and Kara thought she was saved, but he just pressed his weight against the door and looked at Kara with a sad face, as though she was already dead.

Rage poured through her. Idiots. She was giving her life to save these morons, and they wished her dead.

With the soul blade held tightly she turned to face the rats. Five pairs of eyes fixed on her, their hatred reflected in their glowing red eyes. She could feel the dark warlock watching her.

She planted her feet firmly. There was nowhere to run or hide. She would have to stand and fight. The pulsing of the pendant echoed the beating of her heart. She was ready.

The first rat lunged at her throat. With a sideways strike, Kara slashed at the creature's own throat, and it fell at her feet and shrunk back to its normal size. Before she could leap out of the way, another rat jumped on her.

It pinned her to the ground. Its sharp teeth were inches from her face. Desperately, Kara kicked her legs into the creature's sensitive underbelly. Its lips pulled back in a snarl, and it spoke.

"You're finished," said the same voice as before. "Good bye, elemental."

Her breath escaped her suddenly as the weight of two more rats landed on her. White-hot pain surged through her legs, as the rats pulled and bit them. Her heart hit her throat in a loud crunch. Her blade rolled out of her hand. She couldn't move. She couldn't breathe. She couldn't even cry out. Putrid drool fell into her face and she closed her eyes and prepared herself to die...

The pendant pulsed a shockwave through her. Her anger awakened. She wasn't ready to throw in the towel. She tapped into that place deep inside where the power waited.

The subway car shook. She felt a cool wind wash over her. She could smell the earth from the underground tunnels. She could feel the earth's energy like tiny vibrations. Her fingertips tingled. Then her elemental energy rushed through her body like a bolt of lightning. Her muscles tensed. She opened her eyes. When she could contain it no longer, she released her elemental power.

Silver energy exploded from her. The rats flew through the air and smashed into the side of the car with incredible force. Their bodies were wrapped in coils of silver electricity. Their screams resonated and then silence. They fell to the floor, twitched, and then all that was left of them were charred normal-sized rats that looked like burnt toast.

Kara stared at her hands—as a guardian her power had been golden, as a mortal it was silver.

The light in the car flashed on and off and then it exploded. Shards of glass fell from the ceiling like brilliant gems.

Kara wiggled her nose. The scent of burnt flesh filled the compartment as vapors rose from the bodies. She heard the yells from the neighboring wagon and ignored them. She realized that she was shaking, not only because of the cold—but also from fear that she was capable of such enormous destruction. She bent down and picked up her blade.

She could feel the eyes of the people in the next wagon, but she didn't look at them. They had left her for dead.

"Don't leave us here," she heard a man's voice through the glass as he pounded on it. "We saw what you did—you can save us!"

Kara's anger was still fresh. Part of her wanted to punch the man in the face because he was the one who had locked the door. She watched them as they fiddled with the lock.

"ELEMENTAL!"

A thunderous voice reverberated throughout the underground tunnel. Concrete pieces and stone showered the crippled train again. The people in the next wagon screamed and cowered under the seats.

"I WILL KILL YOU!"

She could see streaks of red light bouncing up and down outside. At first she thought they were flashlights, but then she saw that ten giant rats were scurrying towards her car. They were coming for her. If she stayed, the passengers in the next cart would surely die. She couldn't take that chance. The pendant pulled her towards—there was only one thing to do.

Without turning back, Kara sprinted towards the front of the train, jumped down onto the tracks, and bolted into the darkness.

CHAPTER 15

THE MAN ON THE ROOF

KARA RAN WITH ALL the strength she could muster. She could hear the rat's claws tearing up the ground behind her. She could almost feel their foul breath on her neck. As the adrenaline kicked in, she felt a sudden burst of speed and wished she could have been in her M-suit—she knew she couldn't sprint like this for much longer. Sooner rather than later, she would have to turn around and fight for her life.

The pendant hovered in the air before her. Kara felt like she was a dog on a leash going for a run, but she didn't argue with the pendant—it was clear it knew where it was going.

White light appeared suddenly at the end of the tunnel and grew brighter. The walls of the tunnel vibrated. She knew it wasn't the rats—a 400-ton subway train was roaring towards her at thirty-five miles per hour.

In less than seven seconds, it would hit.

But she couldn't stop running. Her momentum pushed her forward. If she tried to stop now, she would fall, and the rats would tear her to pieces.

Six seconds.

She looked from side to side. There were no adjoining tunnels that she could see. There was only straight—or stop and die.

Five seconds.

Kara's legs shook as the adrenaline rush began to fade. She blinked away the sweat that ran into her eyes. Only her fear kept her going now. David's face flashed in her mind's eye. Would he be all right with her gone?

Four seconds.

Her lungs were on fire. She had never run this hard for so long. The train's headlamp turned the tunnel into daylight. The heat from its blinding light felt like it was melting her irises. She'd be blind if she survived.

Three seconds.

If she tripped, she would die.

Two seconds.

She heard her own flesh rip as the burning pain of a rat's claws attacked and numbed her neck. She felt wetness drip down her back. She felt the rat's breath on the back of her head.

One second—

Kara flattened herself against the tunnel wall. The side of the train grazed her cheek as it sped past her. She closed her eyes as a great gust of wind dragged debris and sand down the tracks behind it. She held her breath.

Over the clamor of the metal wheels on metal tracks, she heard the unmistakable crash of flesh against metal.

With a last shake from the powerful wind, the train disappeared into the shadow of the tunnel. Kara was still breathing. She stole a look to her right. Severed rat bodies lay on the tracks. She counted them—they were all there, and very dead.

Shaken but still alive, she felt sorry for the creatures—they had been used.

She glimpsed at her watch. 2:14pm.

She wiped the wind-blown dust from her eyes with her sleeve. Small incandescent lights lined the walls and gave Kara enough light to make out her surroundings. She had to get out of here before the warlock sent more rats after her. The numbness in her neck was making its way down her back. She felt feverish and tried to suppress her shaking. Could you die from a rat bite? As if on cue, she heard the distant tapping sound of four-legged creatures running her way. The pendant pulled her down the tunnel even more frantically. Obediently, Kara forced her legs into a jog. Her throat burned with every breath. She was dizzy from exertion, and her head felt like it was about to explode. She needed to rest.

"You cannot hide, elemental," came a voice from the shadows. "Come out, come out, wherever you are..."

Kara didn't stop. Her jog became a run, but she was running on empty—the thought of seeing David and the others was the only thing that kept her going.

The tunnel walls rippled suddenly as thought they were made of water. They shifted, and Kara found herself running towards a dead end. She was facing a stone wall that hadn't been there a second ago. The walls rippled again, and two new tunnels opened on her left and right. What was happening? Was the rat's poison affecting her?

The pendant pulled her towards the tunnel on the right. The tunnel stretched as she ran, like in those dreams when you're trying to escape, but you're running in slow motion.

Kara turned down yet another tunnel—each time following the pendant's intuition. The tunnels all looked the exact same. Was this a trick? The air was stale, and it stunk of oil. Her head started to spin. She collapsed against the wall and tried to breath. She wiped her clammy palms on her jeans then reached around and touched the back of her neck. When she examined her fingers, they were stained with blood and some green substance.

Forgetting her pain, she pushed herself off and ran blindly up the tunnel. Every step was a blade piercing into the flesh of her back. She thought she saw a light in the distance, and her spirits lifted—but then the light shimmered and vanished. Kara yelled out in frustration. She was running through a labyrinth of underground tunnels that kept shifting and reappearing. She would never get out. If she died down here, her body would never be found.

She staggered forward, then her boot lost solid ground. The next thing she knew, she was falling through a gap in the floor.

She crashed hard on the ground below. Her blade fell from her hand. The paralysis had deadened her legs to the pain from the fall. She dragged herself to a sitting position against the wall and looked around.

She was in another tunnel. Chunks of concrete lay in piles across the tracks and the crumbling graffiti covered walls trickled with water.

She didn't recognize this tunnel. And from the looks of it, it hadn't been used in decades. Kara was lost.

Her throat muscles were numb, and it felt like it was shrinking. Soon it would close up, and she would die of asphyxiation.

She heard a laugh coming from down the tunnel. She didn't even bother to look. She felt worn out. She had failed. David and the others would have to do fight the warlock without her.

She rolled her bracelet between her fingers for comfort. It had brought David luck many times before, but her situation seemed beyond luck or help.

If you can hear me bracelet, I need all the luck you can give me,

Maybe the bracelet just worked for David.

Tiny wind chimes sounded in the distance, and Kara knew she was losing her mind. Her goose down jacket wasn't keeping her warm anymore. She knew the poison was killing her. She stared at her boots and willed them to move. Nothing—it was as though they had melted into the ground and weren't part of her anymore. Her lids fell. She nodded off to sleep.

"What are ya doing up there?" said a voice suddenly.

Kara opened her eyes with a start and looked around. From what she could see, the tunnel was empty. She was hallucinating—a side effect from the rat's poison no doubt.

"Great, I'm hearing voices." She spoke into the darkness and closed her eyes again.

"Voices? You can hear me?" said the voice excitedly.

"Thank the stars! It's been so long since I've had any visitors. The stars were right! Are ya here to buy my latest supply of *Hog Troll Brain ointment?* I brewed a nice batch just yesterday. It goes on smooth—and it's really great against wrinkles. I've used it myself!"

Her lids lifted. The voice sounded so close and somehow it sounded so real.

"Is someone there?" she managed to say, in a scratchy voice.

"Of course there is—there's *you,* and then there's *me,*" said the voice. "And here we are, just the two of us. Hmm—isn't that a song? I swear I've heard that before."

"...but I can't see you." Kara thought the warlock might be playing a trick on her, but she was too exhausted to care. She just wanted to sleep.

"That's because you're up there—and I'm down here," said the voice.

Kara looked around her. She sat against the wall of one of the subway tunnels. Maybe there was another tunnel on a level beneath her? Could the voice be coming from there?

"But where? I still can't see you? If you are a figment of my imagination—you'd think I'd let myself see my own delusions. I'm seriously losing it—"

"Look down," interrupted the voice, a little irritated. It sounded like it was coming from *above* her. But how could that be?

She looked up, and her jaw dropped.

An elderly man was hanging by his feet from the top of the tunnel as though his boots were super-glued to the roof. He wore a dilapidated straw-brown toga-style robe tied in the middle by a leather belt. Tiny bells hung from his belt. His skin was very white, like it hadn't been exposed to the sun in a very long time. He had dark circles under his eyes. His milky-white skin was wrinkled and drooped down like it was melted. He looked like a mixture between a two hundred year old Spiderman —without the red and blue tights) and Albert Einstein. His hair was wiry white, and it stuck out of either side of his head like a giant afro cloud. His beard was braided with colored strings and drooped past his belly. And strangely enough, his hair and clothes didn't seem to be affected by gravity—it was as though he was standing upright, even though Kara was sitting on the ground underneath him? He stood with his hands on his hips, and when he tapped his black wellington rubber boots against the tunnel's roof, his bells rang softly.

"How are you doing that?" asked Kara.

"Doing what?"

"Hanging upside down like that?"

He frowned, and his large bushy eyebrows nearly covered his brown eyes completely.

The man pointed to himself. "*I'm* not hanging upside down...*you* are."

Kara didn't know how to answer that. Was this hallucination all part of the rat's poison? It had to be. She focused on the hanging man and tried not to think about losing her mind.

"I don't know what you mean, but it doesn't matter anymore— I'm hallucinating. You're not really here, and I'm obviously dying.

The rats got me—and now I've ruined everything. I'll never save my mom now."

"RATS!" The man sprinted down the tunnel's ceiling shaking his fist.

"Where are ya rats! Think ya can hide from me! If you think you're going to steal my double-decker club sandwich again, you'll be sorry! I'm going to boil your tails for GLUE!"

The ringing of his tiny bells faded as he disappeared down the tunnel. He ran surprisingly fast for someone so old. Then Kara could hear the bells reverberating and the tapping of footsteps, and the old man reappeared on the ceiling above her.

"Well, I think I've scared them off. They won't be bothering us anymore—rat stew is back on the menu."

The old man examined Kara. "So—which potions are you interested in? I have a fine *Grow-back-your-toenails tonic*, or *Broth of Baboon liver elixir*, or maybe you'd prefer *Blood of a Hag jelly*? I know! You've come to see my house, haven't ya? I've done a lot of updates. I have running water! Can you imagine that?" He clasped his beard excitedly.

Kara stifled a laugh. *I guess this is how crazy people imagine things, since I've seriously lost my mind.*

She looked up at the old man, "Even if I wanted to, I can't walk."

The old man studied her for a moment. "So, if you're not here for my potions, then why are you here? And how is that you can see and hear me, eh? Can ya answer me that?"

Kara let out a painful breath. "I can see you because I'm hallucinating. The thing is—I'm lost, and I've failed the mission. I'll never see my friends again."

It was stupid, but Kara had thought that once the warlock had been defeated, she might finally have a normal life with David. But things didn't always turn out for the best. She reached down and clasped the pendant in her hands. The runes still glowed a soft yellow, as though a fire burned on the inside of the stone.

"Where did ya get that?" The old man's eyes widened. "That's a witch's rune pendant—and a very particular one at that."

"Why? Does it matter?" said Kara. She let go of the pendant. She didn't want to talk about where she got it, because she would have to talk about David and the others, and she didn't feel like it right now.

"Why are you staring at me like that?"

"Well, that explains why ya can see and hear me."

"Huh?"

"Regular folks can't see or hear me. I've cast a magic veil about, I should be invisible to ya—but ya see me. Only those with supernatural abilities can see through the veil—and I can see that you, my dear, have the supernatural about ya."

Kara's neck started to ache from looking up. "So, I'm not hallucinating? You're really up there hanging by your feet."

"The stars have brought ya to me for a reason. It is no coincidence ya ended up in my tunnels. That pendant brought ya here. Tell me—what mission are ya talking about?"

Kara thought she was still hallucinating, but decided to tell the old man anyway. She leaned the back of her head against the wall. She could hardly keep it up anymore. Her eyelids were so heavy.

"Oh, stars! I knew the great ones would need my help! I've been waiting a hundred and fifty years for this!" The old man jumped up and down, and Kara thought he must have been using superglue to stay up like that.

The old man was silent for a moment. "A dark warlock, ya say..." He stroked his beard. "I thought I sensed dark magic. It explains why the tunnels were shifting earlier. I came out to explore, ya see, and there ya were, right here—and ya can see me. It takes a very powerful warlock to channel his power all the way down here—especially into my tunnels. ...curious, I thought they were all dead."

His white puffy hair swayed to the side as he began to scratch the top of his head.

Kara felt that her brain about to explode through her eye sockets. It took all of her energy to keep conversing with the old man. But something nagged at her.

"How...how did you know about dark magic?" Kara suspected that she might not be hallucinating after all.

"What's your name girl?" asked the old man.

"Kara...Kara Nightingale."

"Well, then Kara Nightingale, ya best follow me." The old man turned on his heel and started to walk away in the opposite direction on the tunnel's roof.

Kara shook her head. "Wait, I can't walk. I can't feel my legs. His rats got me—I think their claws had some sort of poison."

She reached down and rubbed her legs, maybe it would help the circulation. "I can't feel anything anymore, I think it's killing me—"

"Wait here! I've just the thing." The old man rocketed down the tunnel, his bells resonating behind him. He reappeared a minute later with a vial in his hand. "Here, drink this—all of it."

Kara examined the vial of bright orange liquid. She popped the corked top off with her thumb and drank it down. It was thick, hard to swallow, and tasted like tar.

"Yuck!" she coughed. "Tastes like sewer gunk. What is that?"

"One of my better potions," said the old man happily. "It's an antidote against dark magic—a tonic against dark venom in particular. Not to worry—you'll feel better in a jiffy."

All at once Kara felt the effects of the potion. It was warm and moved down her throat slowly, like thick pea soup. Warmth gushed from her neck all the way down to her toes. Her skin prickled, and she felt her muscles come back to life, like frozen meat starting to thaw. She took a deep breath and wiggled her legs. Soon, all the pain had disappeared. She felt renewed. She felt strong again. She felt like she'd just woken up from a long sleep.

Kara stood up and steadied herself. "Thank you, I feel better already." She rubbed her head. "And my headache's gone too."

After a quick search of the grounds, she found her soul blade and sheathed it back inside her jacket. She looked up and saw that the old man was smiling down at her.

"Who are you?" But as soon as she asked the question, she already knew the answer.

The old man grinned. "I'm Gideon Magius, the witch doctor. The stars have spoken, Kara, and I'm going to help ya defeat the dark warlock."

CHAPTER 16

A MAGICAL ALLIANCE

KARA SPRINTED DOWN THE tunnel to keep up with Gideon. It was the weirdest thing—chasing an old man with a white afro who ran upside down along the dark ceiling of an abandoned New York subway tunnel. Gravity had new meaning for Kara. Only a witch doctor could run upside down. She had no idea what a witch doctor was, or what they did, but she was very grateful his disgusting orange tonic had cured her.

Gideon had explained to her that he was on another *magical plane,* and that on that plane he was right side up, and therefore Kara was, in fact, upside down. She decided not to press the matter. He had made it clear to her that she needed his help, and Olga had said the same.

After running down the tunnel's grime and through strange wet puddles that Kara would rather not think about, they reached Gideon's house. And of course it was upside down.

It was the weirdest house Kara had ever seen. It was nestled on the ceiling of the tunnel. Its orange walls appeared to be made of canned goods and metal plates, and it had a row of round windows on the roof. It looked like a mix between a space ship and a gigantic pumpkin.

Gideon disappeared behind the front door. He reappeared moments later with a wooden staff that had bells attached to it, and with a selection of leather pouches that hung from the leather belt around his waist. He had also wrapped an old fur cloak around his shoulders. The poor foxes' heads leaned across his shoulders, their glass eyes fixed on Kara. She cringed but decided not to say anything about how wrong it was to wear fur nowadays.

Gideon beamed at Kara. "Here we are. I'm ready to rid the world of this dark business. I might be a little rusty—but I'm sure it'll all come back to me if the stars want it to."

Gideon strolled towards her with a spring in his step. His pouches bounced around his belt.

"Uh...Gideon, you think you can come down on *my* plane for a while? I think I've twisted the muscles in my neck from staring up all the time."

The witch doctor smiled. "Stars! But of course! I can see how having us both on the same plane would make matters simpler." He snapped his fingers and with a puff of white smoke, he landed with a thud beside Kara. "Is that better?"

"Yes, thank you," said Kara. He was a head taller than she when he stood beside her.

"I'm supposed to rendezvous with my team on the corner of Broadway and 42nd street at around 3:00 pm. So, if you're ready, we really should be going."

Gideon's smile disappeared. "Oh yes, the spirit walkers. Such unnatural creatures, you're lucky Olga didn't vaporize them or cook them into her famous Spicy Spirit Stew."

Kara frowned and wondered if that was what Olga had been sautéing in her cauldron.

"They're not *unnatural*. They're my friends—*and* guardian angels—*and* they're trying to help us fight the dark warlock. They're on our side, you know. I care about them." Kara fought to control her irritation.

"The dead should stay dead," said the witch doctor matter-of-factly.

"So...how come the legion doesn't know about you?" said Kara, trying to change the subject. "You obviously have magic."

"The legion? You mean that interfering spirit-walker legion? Why would they? They're nothing to me. I'm just a witch doctor. I can do a few basic spells, like cast a veil, but I mostly create remedies to protect others against dark magic. I'm more of a potions master. That's what witch doctors do—make magical medicine. I'm not powerful enough to be considered a real threat to anyone."

He frowned, and when he spoke again his voice was full of contempt. "I don't care for the dealings of the spirit walkers—I'm sorry to say."

Kara decided to drop the topic. It was no use arguing with a stubborn old man, who probably hadn't had a conversation with a real person in years. And she needed his help to find the way out of the underground subway tunnels. She looked down the tunnel. "So, how do we get to 42nd street from here?"

Gideon's smile returned. "Easy, I know a shortcut. I know all the secret passageways down in the tunnels. I've lived down here for over a hundred years. This way."

He walked down the tunnel talking to himself and counting the walls.

Kara laughed and ran to join him. They walked side by side for a few minutes until they reached another tunnel that crossed their path.

A sinister laugh echoed throughout the tunnel.

Kara froze mid-step.

Suddenly, the walls of the tunnel shifted and instead of an opening, they stood facing another wall.

"Oh, ya want to try that again, do ya?" Gideon reached into one of the pouches on his belt and then threw a handful of red powder at the wall.

"To the stars!" he shouted. The stone wall shifted and disappeared. The same tunnel stretched out before them again.

"Come, come, before the tunnels change again." Gideon raced down the tunnel like a wild man being chased by a tiger.

Kara started to follow him but halted.

Six creatures stepped from the shadows at the edge of the tunnel. They had eight scaly legs and tails like scorpions. They were the size of small ponies. Their sharp venomous claws ripped the ground under their feet. They smashed their tails against the walls and shattered the rock like it was made of soft clay. Their glowing red eyes were focused on Kara. Glowing runes covered their backs, and the smell that rolled off of them was a mixture of sulfur and bile.

Gideon screamed and jumped back, swishing his staff before him.

"Get back, you devils!"

He tripped on his own legs and went down. Desperately, he pulled at one of the bags around his waist. "Don't come any closer, or I'll turn ya into a bowl of spider chowder!"

Kara pulled out her blade and ran towards the old man. She reached down and pulled him up just in time to avoid being skewered by one of the insects' scorpion tails as it pierced the ground a centimeter from her boot. They dashed down the tunnel with the giant spiders scurrying after them.

Kara stopped and turned around to face their attackers. Her soul blade twinkled in the yellow light. Six against two—it wasn't fair, the odds weren't good. She knew her only chance was to act quickly. She didn't have time to think of a plan. Her instincts just kicked in.

One of the giant spiders charged at Kara, its tail slashing side to side, aiming at her head. She ducked and swung her blade towards the underbelly. As soon as the blade touched the soft tissue, green ooze spluttered to the ground and splattered in Kara's face. The spider shimmered and shrunk back to the size of Kara's palm. The runes disappeared.

In the corner of her eye she saw Gideon throw a red vial at one of the creatures. It exploded in a ball of liquid red fire on contact.

The spider wailed and flung its charred body against the wall of the tunnel, convulsing. It slumped to the side, and then it keeled over and shrunk back to its normal size. The witch doctor rushed over and stomped the spider repeatedly with his rubber boots.

Gideon prepared a new tonic as another oversized spider advanced in his direction. Two more spiders launched their attack on Kara. She stepped back, rolled to the side and swung her blade into the first creature's head with a satisfying crack. She tried to retrieve her blade in time to fight the second—but not fast enough. With a powerful whack from one of its legs, it caught Kara in the chest, and she went crashing into the wall with a horrible crunch. The force squeezed the breath out of her.

She scrambled to her feet, her vision blurred from knocking her head on the wall. She stood there breathing hard. She couldn't tell whether two spiders were coming at her or one. She blinked. The spider's eight glowing red eyes burned with hatred. It opened its mandibles and a glowing green web shot from its maw. Kara leaped to the side, but too late. It caught her in mid-stride and flung her around. She crashed on the ground. Her arms and legs were pinned awkwardly to her sides by the sticky web. Green vapors rose from it, and the smell of sulfur burned her nose. She couldn't move. She could hear Gideon yell as he fought the other spider.

A hairy-scaled leg rolled her over, so that the giant spider's ugly face was a few inches from her own.

"Ah...a little help here, Gideon," she called, her pulse racing. No answer.

The spider opened its maw to bite off her head. Her fear quickly turned to anger. Her instincts kicked it, and a cool energy surged through her, wanting to be released. She was buzzing inside. Her hair lifted on end. The ground groaned beneath her. And then the air around her was alive with electricity.

The spider lowered its head.

Crack!

An electric silver bolt shot out of Kara and blinded her for a second. The creature wailed—then quiet, nothing but the smell of burnt hair. A blob of green ooze sizzled and popped on the ground. A single tiny leg was all that remained of the giant spider.

She moved her arms and legs. She checked herself. The web had melted away; only a few sticky green fragments remained as stains on her jacket. She stood up. The electricity was still vigorous inside her, and the pendant pulsed.

"Now that is power." Gideon smiled as he adjusted one of the pouches around his belt. Kara spotted the last spider, squished like a rotten tomato behind him.

"Never saw anything like it before, and I've seen a many great things in my time, so the stars can tell ya. Your magic is quite extraordinary—powers from mother earth materialize as silver electricity from your fingers—beautiful and deadly. And that's what it's going to take to bring down the dark warlock."

Kara didn't feel very powerful at the moment. She knew they were wasting precious time. The dark warlock kept throwing obstacles in her way. He was hoping to keep them down here for a while, even if he couldn't kill them. She knew what he was planning.

She searched the ground with her boots and bent down to retrieve her blade. It was covered in green slime. It was disgusting—but it was the only weapon she had, so she wiped the blade on her jeans and put it in her belt again.

She looked up. "Let's get out of here before more giant insects decide to make us lunch."

Gideon nodded, his white hair bounced on the top of his head. "Agreed. This way."

They ran down the tunnel and up a slope. Kara could hear and feel the vibrations of subway trains. Gideon led her down two more tunnels, turned right, waited for a train to pass, then ran up to the platform. Kara kept up with him, but her rapid breaths were like razor blades in her throat. They climbed up the platform and hoped no one had spotted them. This was New York after all. There were more bizarre things in this gigantic city than a scrawny teenaged girl covered in dirt and blood climbing out of a subway tunnel. She figured she would blend in just fine.

Her jeans were stained with her own blood, and she did her best to cover herself with her jacket. As they made their way across to the exits, Kara couldn't help but notice the strange looks she and Gideon were getting—mostly the witch doctor. His big hair and strange attire called for attention. Kara hoped they wouldn't attract the wrong attention—getting stopped by the cops now would stop the mission. They couldn't afford hiccups of any kind.

The sign above the two tall glass exit doors read *42nd street*. Kara pushed open the doors and stepped onto the sidewalk.

42nd Street towered over them. Billboards with screens the size of small shops lined the streets that thronged with locals and tourists. She smelled roasted peanuts and asphalt.

But there was something very different this time.

A green glowing mist on the ground slipped through the crowds. It snaked around cars and avoided buildings. Stealthy, it crept along the street. Searching tendrils rose from the mist and coiled around a young man. It enveloped him like a cocoon and strands of it disappeared into the man's mouth. The next moment, the mist reappeared with a brilliant white sphere. His soul, Kara realized in horror. Hundreds of these brilliant spheres floated in the mist and disappeared out of sight like runway lights in a fog. The young man's skin started to glow with green runes, but he kept walking—oblivious to the fact that his soul had just been stolen.

The mist crept back onto the ground and launched itself at its next victim.

"Oh dear! May the stars help us," said Gideon.

Kara could hardly breathe. "What is that mist? It's taking their souls."

Gideon lowered his head. "That, my dear, is shadow mist—dark warlock mist. It is dark magic of the worse kind. Only a powerful warlock, rotten to the core, can conjure it. He uses it to steal souls. We're dealing with a madman."

"It's everywhere. We have to stop it!" Kara started forward, but Gideon held her back.

"There's nothing ya can do to stop it now. If the mist touched ya, you'd lose your soul, too."

"So what can we do?"

"We must stop the connection—kill the warlock, and the mist will disappear."

Kara watched in silence as the shadow mist rolled through the crowds, sucked out their souls, and left them like broken shells. Their expressions became sullen, and Kara knew they would sicken and die without their souls—just like her mother.

The shadow mist flowed their way. In a minute or two it would be upon them.

"We cannot stay here for very long," said Gideon. He hit his staff three times on the cement sidewalk. "I don't want that nasty thing near me."

Kara glanced at her watch: 3:05 p.m.

Where were David and the others? She wasn't that late, David would surely have waited for her?

"Well, I must say things have changed since the last time I was up here." Gideon's eyes bulged as he stared at the billboards and skyscrapers. "These tall buildings weren't there in my days." He poked his fingers in his ears. "And it's very loud!"

Kara felt sorry for Gideon. 42nd street must be quite a contrast to his solitary world. She looked up at the sky. It was snowy, overcast and grey. Normally Kara would have thought this was beautiful, but the darkening sky meant that it would soon be dark—the warlock was going begin his ritual.

Her heart raced.

"The warlock has been busy here," said Gideon, watching the crowds like Kara. "We've already lost more souls than I can count—terrible business this is, just terrible."

A dark grey cloud moved unnaturally fast towards the city. Sundown was rapidly approaching—and Kara still had no idea how to defeat the warlock.

"We must act quickly," said Gideon and shook her out of her trance. "He will begin his ceremony at sundown. We will defeat the dark warlock together."

She looked at the old man. "But how? If he's as powerful as you say he is, how can we do it?"

"Just as the witches and witch doctors have done before. We must join our strengths together. I will do what I can—but it is *you* who must defeat him. I am not as powerful as you. Your powers are the key to his destruction. It's the only way, Kara."

Kara shifted nervously.

"These powers of mine as not as simple to conjure as you think. As a guardian angel I got used to them, and after a while I was able to control them. But now, in this body, I'm a complete mess. It's like I've forgotten how to do it. They're different somehow."

The old witch doctor smiled warmly. "That's normal. It's just harder to channel your power as a mortal than a spirit walker. Humans are born with a barrier that keeps them from being in touch with the other supernatural planes. They live on one plane only, while witches and warlocks can access all the planes and get power from each of them."

Gideon looked at Kara. "But you're unique. You're more sensitive to the different planes—like a witch, but differently, in a more organic way. Your use of the earth's energies. Your power is in the earth. You were born with the ability to summon it. Ya just need to focus harder on channeling it. Didn't Olga teach ya how to channel your power? She gave ya her pendant."

Kara looked to the ground. She couldn't meet his eyes.

"There's something I haven't told you about Olga." She told him how the dark warlock had found them out and killed Olga. When she was finished she looked up, but Gideon had turned his back and was silent. She wished she could have saved the old witch. Perhaps she should have tried harder.

"Kara!"

Kara turned towards the voice. Her heart tried to jump out of her chest.

David squeezed through the crowded sidewalk. His radiant smile sent butterflies into her stomach. She felt weak at the knees. His dazzling angel skin was hard to look at. She did her best to suppress her emotions and to act normally. She rolled her leather bracelet around in her fingers. It *had* brought her luck.

"Sorry we're late," said David as he planted himself at her side. He went to grab her hand, but stopped and raked his hair instead. He looked to the ground awkwardly. "Someone messed up back at CDD and Vega'd us to 48th street instead of 42nd."

Jenny appeared seconds later and smiled when she saw Kara.

"And we've been trying to avoid touching the weird green mist that's all over the city," she continued. "I know we're in our M-suits, but I still don't trust it."

"Hey watch it!" She yelled at a man who had knocked into her. She steadied her bow and quiver behind on her back.

Kara searched over their heads. "Where's Peter?"

Jenny's smile disappeared. "He...he had to stay a little longer in the Healing-Xpress than the rest of us. Peter was really in bad shape."

Jenny's voice cracked. "They say it's a miracle his soul survived the jump back to Horizon. They'll have to grow back his angel legs." She wrinkled her brow as she stared at Kara's pants. "What happened to you? You're covered in blood!"

Kara tried to brush it off. "It's nothing, just a few giant warlock rats and big ugly spiders."

"What warlock rats?" David leaned in and inspected her. "Are you still hurt? What about those headaches and nose bleeds?"

Kara avoided his eyes. "No more headaches, actually—Gideon helped me out."

Gideon turned at the mention of his name. They all noticed the old witch doctor for the first time. Jenny laughed softly to herself.

"Who's grandpa?" said David raising his brows as he stared at the fur cloak. "I'm pretty sure Broadway is that way, old man. I believe they're doing a new version of *Cats*."

"I don't like your tone, spirit walker," said Gideon. He frowned, and then he moved his fingers in the air as though he was doing some wacky sign language to fight off the evil spirits. "Yes, I know what you are. I might not have the magic of a warlock, but I can still see through *your* veil. Ya should show more respect to the living. This is *our* realm."

"Look who's talking," snickered David. "You look about to kick over anytime—"

"David." Kara glared at him. "This is Gideon, the one Olga told me to look for. He's a witch doctor, and I owe him my life. We need his help on this mission."

David leaned closer to Kara. "What happened to you after we were separated?" He looked into Kara's eyes. "Tell me."

After she had explained what had transpired in the tunnels, David's demeanor quickly changed. He patted the witch doctor on his fur jacket. "Well, at least you're on our side, gramps." He made a face and picked some fur from his fingers.

Gideon's eyes widened, and he backed away from David, clearly not happy to have been touched by a spirit walker. He did some more signing with his fingers towards David. Then he said, "The shadow mist is approaching, we must leave now."

A shadow passed over Manhattan and Kara knew that time was running out.

Kara stared at her watch. "It's 3:15. Sundown is at exactly 4:39. That gives us just about an hour and a half to find Cleopatra's Needle—and by some miracle defeat the Dark warlock."

"Any ideas how we're going to do that?" asked David.

Kara shrugged. "I guess it'll come to me when we find this place."

"But where do we begin?" said Jenny looking nervous. "New York is one of the biggest metropolises in the world, how are we supposed to find Cleopatra's Needle? And what the heck is it anyway?"

"That's simple," interrupted Gideon. "It's an ancient monument of incredible power. And it's in Central Park."

CHAPTER 17

CLEOPATRA'S NEEDLE

KARA STARED AT THE old man dumbfounded. "Central Park?"

"That's what I said," said Gideon in a nonchalant way. He leaned on his staff.

David and Kara shared a look. "Can you give more information, Gramps? Like—where it is in Central Park? You know how *big* the park is?"

The witch doctor turned and pointed eastward. "It's the obelisk in Central Park. There is only one and quite easy to find."

"So...what is this obelisk?" asked Kara.

The witch doctor squared his shoulders. "The ancient artifact was commissioned by Pharaoh Thutmosis III around 1450 BC in celebration of his 3rd jubilee or the 30th year of his reign. Two of these obelisks were constructed and around 13 or 12BC—I can't remember exactly—they were transported from Heliopolis to Alexandria. The Khedive of Egypt separated the pair in the late

19th century. He sent one to London and another to New York City, both in exchange for aid in modernizing his country."

Kara was speechless. She had had no idea that something so old and precious was in a New York City park.

"It has its own primeval power," continued Gideon. "It is extremely dangerous. Think of it as a giant electrical transformer. The warlock will use the obelisk to amplify his power. It will make him a hundred times more powerful."

"Great, that's just what we needed," said David.

Gideon ignored David and looked to Kara more intensely. "He will use the obelisk's power to summon his minions at sundown today, the winter solstice. If we don't stop him—nothing pure or good will remain on earth."

"You're just full of joy, grandpa." David looked at Kara. "We'll get there faster if we grab a cab."

Kara nodded. "You're right. Let's grab a cab."

David jumped to the side of the street and hailed a yellow cab. Gideon refused to sit next to the spirit walkers and he climbed in the front passenger seat. He was oblivious to the strange looks the cabby was giving him. The cab smelled strongly of cigarette smoke and dirty socks. David's leg brushed up against Kara's, and the blood rushed to her face. From the corner of her eye she could see him staring, but she kept looking straight.

"Central Park, please," she said. She could feel her ears burning. "Uh—near the obelisk?" Kara wasn't sure the driver would know what Cleopatra's Needle was or where it would be.

The cab driver turned on his meter. "I know where that is. It's that tall pointy thing. I'll drop you off on the corner of 81st Street and Fifth Avenue. You can see it from there."

They all scrambled into the cab just as a tidal wave of green mist surged down 42nd street and engulfed everyone out in the open.

The cab ride was longer than Kara had anticipated. Traffic was congested. By the time they had arrived at 81st Street, and David had paid for the fare, Kara's chest was about to explode from nerves. She felt electrified.

4:03 pm. They had approximately half an hour left. Her insides churned, and she fought to control her panic.

Kara turned towards the enormous park. The metal benches and wrought iron gates that lined the outer walls of the park were blanketed in snow. It was a winter wilderness steps away from the busy city. And through the trees in the distance stood the giant obelisk in all its splendor. It looked more like a giant pencil than a needle.

Thunder rolled in the distance. It was loud and unnatural for this time of year. Darkness was quickly approaching. The carpet of green fog that covered the city would soon reach Central Park.

They started down the snowy pathway. Kara stopped and turned. "Gideon? Are you coming?"

The witch doctor stood by the metal gates and rang some of the bells on his belt. His expression was a mixture of determination and fear. "There is a great evil here. We must be vigilant—the dark warlock knows we are here. It's too late to hide from him now—he has seen us—he is watching us right now."

"Well that's just great," grumbled David.

Gideon raised his staff. "We are about to enter the warlock's lair. Be on your guard, spirit walkers, he will strike at us hard. May the stars help us."

Kara walked towards Gideon. "Then we will fight him face to face, and do our best."

She couldn't shake the feeling that they were walking into a trap.

Suddenly the old man grabbed Kara's hand. His icy fingers were as strong as iron, and Kara couldn't pull away. He shook his staff, and his bells rang hypnotically.

Images suddenly started to play inside Kara's head—cities burning; creatures of the darkness roaming the streets; demons sprouting up from the Netherworld; howls of dying mortals as demons and warlock creatures join forces to massacre them; warlocks at the head of government; demons enslaving, chaining and whipping humans; forests burning—the earth charred and barren like a desert.

Kara became conscious of the bells again, and then the images faded.

Kara shook free from Gideon's grip. "What...what was that?"

Gideon's face fell. "That is what will come to pass if ya don't stop him." He paused for a moment. "When the time is right, ya must do as I say. Ya must strike him down when I tell ya."

Kara stared at her open hands. "But my power isn't like a gun. I can't just pull the trigger, and it goes off. It's not like yours. I don't have it bottled up in a vial that I can throw. It doesn't work like that. Gideon, what if I can't do this? What if it doesn't work?"

The old man's brown eyes gleamed. "But it will. It must. Think of your power as a light. When the darkness approaches from the outside, you must resist it. You must destroy it with your light—the light within you. Your power is your light. Let it light up the darkness. The warlock pulls his magic strength from the depths of darkness. And darkness can only be defeated by light."

Kara nodded, but she only understood part of what the old man said. Whatever light she had—she prayed it would be enough.

"Ya must draw strength from the pendant. It is the light when you are in darkness. Ya know it's in there. The pendant will help ya."

As the old man walked away to join the others, Kara held the pendant in her hand. It was a lot warmer now, hot to the touch like it had been sitting on a hot stove. Was that a warning sign? It had been acting up since they got closer to the park. She ran to catch up to the others, and together they entered the park.

It was like stepping into a holiday card. Normally, Kara would have found the snow in the park beautiful, but she felt numb. Her nerves were shot. Her mind was loud with worry. She didn't think she could pull this off.

"Keep your eyes open for anything *magical*," said David, waving his soul blade through the falling snowflakes.

As they ventured further in the park, the obelisk stood out like a giant amongst the trees. Its grey stone frame contrasted against the winter white background. She could see it clearly now. There was no sign of the warlock anywhere, or anything magical. The shadow mist hadn't touched the park yet. She felt like she was walking into an ambush. It was less than twenty minutes to sundown—where was the warlock?

Tall lampposts flickered, and the lights came on as the grey skies darkened. The park was unusually deserted for a winter day like this. It should have been crawling with families with their kids making snowmen and snow angels. Kara scouted the grounds. They only footprints in the snow were their own. Something wasn't right.

"Something feels wrong," said Jenny, as though reading Kara's thoughts. "Where are all the people—?"

"Duck!" David dropped on his belly behind a rise of snow. Kara and the others followed his example. She peered over the edge of the snow bank.

Two hundred yards beyond the clearing, six dark robed figures walked towards the obelisk. Slowly they formed a circle around the ancient monument. Their faces were covered by their hoods, and Kara couldn't tell which one was the dark warlock—they were identical in every way. Then they all lifted their arms and chanted in a language Kara didn't recognize. The chanting grew louder and reverberated around them as though it had been amplified.

Then a shimmering green mist coiled around their hands like glowing ribbons. The mist shot from their hands and hit the obelisk. The ground shook. The obelisk groaned as the mist spiraled around it, then the mist disappeared as though the obelisk had consumed it. The great stone began to gleam green, like a giant toxic cucumber.

Kara's pulse raced. The ritual had already begun.

David lowered his voice. "Did Ariel forget to tell us a crucial piece of information—like that there are *six* freaking warlocks and not just one? What are we supposed to do now?"

"We need a diversion," Kara decided. "If we can draw half the group out into the park, we will have a better chance fighting them if they're separated. I think the real Dark warlock, whoever he is, will stay near the obelisk. He won't leave it."

Kara didn't want to face six warlocks as a mortal. It terrified her, but she didn't see any other way.

"She's right," said Gideon, scowling at the warlocks in the clearing. "The Dark warlock will stay and perform the ritual. He will not stray from the obelisk when the hour is near. He will not take that chance—he needs the power of the obelisk."

"Okay then," agreed David, "sounds like we have a plan. I know of a few ways to get the warlocks to chase me, and it's not with my pretty face."

Jenny crawled closer to the edge. "No, it's because you're a moron. But you'll still need my help, pretty boy."

David smiled impishly. "Jenny and I will be your distraction. We'll draw them out over to that little bridge over there and keep them busy. That should give you and Gideon enough time to take care of the dark warlock."

He twirled a soul blade skillfully between his fingers like a baton. "I'm feeling out of practice—I need to kill something."

Kara turned to the others to speak, but her mouth wouldn't open. Could she really defeat a warlock?

"Fight magic with magic," whispered Kara to no one in particular. She felt a gentle squeeze on her arm and turned to see Gideon's smiling eyes.

David watched her. "The sun's almost gone, we have to hurry."

Kara's fingers dug into the snow. "Be careful, something feels off. I still have a feeling it's a trap."

Jenny crawled out of the warlocks' sight and stood up. "At the rate we're going, traps are our lot in life—we're used to them by now. You be careful, too."

"I'll be fine, it's you two I'm worried about." Kara did her best to sound determined. What choice did she have? She couldn't let her friends down.

David stood next to Jenny. "The show's starting. Come on, let's go."

"Uh...guys...where's Gideon?" Kara wiped the snow from her face and searched the grounds. "He's gone!" She turned on the spot and whispered. "Gideon? Gideon!"

"I'm telling you, gramps is off to Broadway or something," said David. "That was his one act—the disappearing grandpa act."

Kara studied the snow around her. She could see Gideon's tracks. They led away from them. But how could that be? She followed the tracks.

"What the...?" She knelt down and brushed the snow with her hand. Gideon's tracks stopped suddenly. Could witch doctors fly? Had he gone into another supernatural plane? It made no sense.

David looked amused. "It's not funny."

"The old fart abandoned us."

"No, he wouldn't do that. But something's off. How could he have just disappeared like that—?"

Kara tensed. "Did you guys hear that?"

Strange howls pierced the cold air.

"What...what was that?" Kara looked over her shoulder. "That sounded really close."

David stood by her side. His blade trembled in his hand. "I don't know, but I do know that there aren't any wolves in New York."

Jenny nocked *her arrow* and drew back the taut string of *her bow*. "Whatever they are, they don't sound very friendly."

Kara had the horrible feeling that something terrible had happened to Gideon. The winds suddenly wailed like the howling of beasts. Snowflakes melted on her hot face, and she saw red eyes glowing faintly through the falling snow.

A dozen creatures emerged from the snowstorm, as though the snow itself had molded them. They were massive. At first Kara thought they were polar bears, but she quickly realized her mistake. They had muscular upper bodies like apes, but with a row of icy spikes sticking out from their hunched backs. They flexed the shiny black claws that protruded from their large furry paws, and their razor-sharp fangs gleamed. They looked like a cross between abominable snowmen and albino wolves on steroids.

They moved effortlessly and soundlessly through the snow, as though they were gliding over it. Their thick white fur was a perfect camouflage in the winter-white background. Their long purple tongues flicked out of their enormous maws, like packman mouths that opened all the way back to their necks. They circled around the group, boxing them in like a pride of lions around their prey. Kara and her friends were lunch.

David stood protectively in front of Kara. "Looks like the Bronx zoo had a sale on big white ugly beasts."

The creatures snarled as though they understood David. Ice and snow fell from their thick hides. The white beasts stood and waited. Unnatural intelligence glistened in their eyes. Kara's heart pulsed in her throat.

Green runes rippled through their white fur, and Kara knew instantly what they were. "This is the dark warlock's doing. They have the same markings as the other creatures. They're his."

"I don't care who they belong to," said David. "If they come any closer—I'm going to skin them."

Hatred flashed in the beasts' red eyes. Then they lunged.

"Stick together!" David ran and met their onslaught head on.

He swung his blade skillfully at a giant white beast. Before it had time to react, he sliced the creature's stomach with an upward stroke. It crumbled into a white powder at his feet, shimmered, and then disintegrated into snow and blew away.

David stood shocked for a moment. But as he turned, another creature jumped him—and he disappeared under the heavy hide of the beast.

"David!" Kara pulled her soul blade from her jacket and charged forward. She didn't have time to think about how small her blade was compared to those giant snow beasts—she just ran. She had to save David.

Two howling snow beasts blocked her way. They bared their gleaming fangs.

Kara skidded to a stop and readied herself.

She heard a cackling sound over the wind, as though the creatures were laughing at her. The first creature lowered its head and crept closer. It jumped out for her, and Kara crowned it with the base of the dagger. Its head fell sideways with a loud crack, and it fell. She kicked it to make sure it wasn't moving.

A massive blow hit her from behind, and she staggered forward. She turned into the thrashing arms of another creature. It hit her in the chest and knocked the breath out of her. She cried out and nearly dropped her blade. As its fangs grazed her throat, she stabbed the creature in the neck with a downward stroke. It disintegrated with a pop.

Kara screamed frantically for David. She could see him trying to fight his way out of the crowd of beasts that surrounded him. He used his elbows like a seasoned soldier. He knocked one in the face and then stabbed it in the head. It withered and disintegrated. With an upward swing, he sliced through another creature's neck, decapitating it. It disappeared with a frosty flash.

More snow beasts emerged from the blizzard. Kara was trapped.

They leaped.

She faked to her left, then swiveled and jumped out of the way, kicking out with her legs. She heard a satisfying crunch, but she wasn't fast enough. As she jumped up from the ground, a burning pain exploded on her left arm, and white feathers from her jacket flew into the air. She felt the wetness of her blood. But she couldn't stop and look at her injury.

A powerful hit caught her in the side, and Kara went down. Instinctively, she rolled and pushed herself up just in time to avoid a big white paw that smashed the snow where her head had been seconds before. She grasped her blade and thrust it with all her strength into the creature's head. The beast toppled over and pinned Kara to the ground for a moment. Its weight crushed her and its putrid smell choked her. The creature's body shimmered and vanished into snow. She breathed again.

She saw two white beasts charge at Jenny. She released her arrow, ducked sideways, and nocked a second arrow even as the first one pierced the snow beast's chest. She released it and hit a second beast. But the arrows didn't seem to have much of an effect on them, except to make them angrier. The creatures came thrashing at Jenny. They knocked her bow out of her hands, and she staggered back.

She was surrounded. They were going to tear her apart.

Kara struggled to her feet and jumped to Jenny's aid. Something hard crashed into her, and she fell on her back. Pressure crushed her chest, and her cry died in her throat. She looked up. The massive jaws of a beast were poised to bite off her head. She winced at its putrid breath. Its purple tongue flicked out of its chops, and warm drool dribbled onto her face. But it didn't attack.

"Well. Well. Well—what do we have here?"

Kara recognized the voice and the cruel blue eyes of the girl immediately. She wore a white down coat with a fox-fur hood and knee-high white leather boots. Her long white-blonde hair waved behind her in the wind like a cape. Her pointy features were twisted in a fake smile.

"Hello, sister dear," said Lilith in a pleasant voice. "Didn't expect to see me again, did you?"

CHAPTER 18

CHANNELING

KARA'S ANGER ERUPTED. "Lilith! I've should have known you'd be involved in something like this."

Kara tried to move out from under the drooling creature, but it was like trying to move a car.

Lilith laughed. "I guess you wish you had killed me when you had the chance—right? But you couldn't, could you—your pathetic conscience wouldn't let you. It's always been your greatest weakness—so totally predictable—you're just so *good*. It's sickening."

Kara struggled under the snow beast's weight. She felt warm liquid trickle from down her left eyebrow.

"What's this?" Lilith bent down and traced her finger on Kara's forehead. "Blood? You're mortal? Yes, I see it now—you're not a glowing puppet like them."

Lilith stood up and shook her head. "Tut-tut-tut, how delightfully perfect. It'll be even easier to kill you, and this time you'll stay dead. Your cursed angel soul is going to die tonight, dearest sister, along with your angel friends. I can't say I feel sorry. Nope. It's time for you to feel the pain and suffering that I did in this blood—bag of a body. You're going to pay dearly for doing this to me."

Kara glowered. "I didn't do anything to you—you did it to yourself. What are you doing here anyway? I thought you'd be in a girl's correction facility or something."

Lilith's red lips spread into a smile. "I broke out of that easily after I was caught robbing a jewelry store, then a Mercedes Benz, and after that a few ATMs. Those stupid mortals weren't very happy when I got my hands on a few automatic weapons."

"News flash—you're a mortal too."

Lilith's smile disappeared. "Yes, an unfortunate oversight thanks to you, but not for long."

Kara screwed up her face. "What? What are you talking about?"

Her half-sister ignored her and called out to the snow beast. "Bring the others. It's time."

The snow beast released Kara, and she gladly filled her lungs with air. She winced as she stood up. She knew she had a few bruised or broken ribs, but she was still alive.

Something hit her in the back, and she staggered forward. The snow beast prodded her with its nose, urging her forward.

David and Jenny stumbled beside her, each with a snow creature nudging them on. Jenny turned around and punched the creature on its snout. The beast retaliated with a powerful blow to her head and knocked her to the ground. Cursing loudly Jenny struggled to her feet, more angry than hurt.

David's expression darkened at the sight of Lilith. "Well, isn't it my favorite albino-Barbie? I thought you'd joined the freak show by now. But I guess the circus couldn't fit you in between The Elephant Man and The Four legged Lady. I thought you'd make a splendid Queen of the Freaks."

Lilith giggled and raked her long blonde hair with her fingers. "I knew you'd tag along, David McGowan. You always seem to appear whenever I have dealings with my sister."

"I'm like a bad habit—I always turn up."

"Take their weapons. Search them."

The beasts obediently took away their soul blades and Jenny's bow and quiver with the few arrows she had left.

With a red manicured finger, Lilith counted their heads. "Aren't you missing someone? Yes, the boy with the glasses—the mousy looking one. Didn't something unfortunate happen to him?" she laughed.

"Shut up," growled Jenny, "Don't say another word."

Lilith raised her brows at Jenny, a hint of a smile on her face. "Ah yes, Janet. I see you still have that abominable purple hair."

She inspected Jenny more closely. "You'd think the angel legion would have had higher standards. You look so *trashy*—with that hair and those clothes. I'm surprised they let you out looking like that."

Jenny glared at her and said in an icy tone. "The legion isn't *shallow* and *fake* like you—they don't care what we look like, as long as we do our jobs."

"I can *see* that." Lilith grinned wickedly. "But don't worry, you won't be an angel for much longer."

She snapped her fingers. "Come along, Wergoth would like a word." She strolled ahead of them.

The snow creatures pushed them along behind her. David and Kara shared a look. Her heart rang in her ears, and she shook her head with dread.

"Lilith, please tell me you didn't..."

Lilith laughed and kicked some snow with her boot. "But of course I did—what did you expect? That I'd stay in this pathetic disgusting weak mortal body? Never. I did what I needed to do to get back to my home, to where I belong."

Kara stumbled forward, numb from the realization of what her half-sister had done. Jenny looked confused, and she mouthed the word *what?*

"Lilith...what did you do?" her voice came out as a whisper of desperation.

Lilith turned her head as she walked. "When I was transformed into this disgusting human body, I still had remnants of my superb demonic self—I could still see and sense my servants, just as I can see angels and other supernatural elements. They called out to me. I knew I couldn't stay in this weak shell—I needed to do something. I needed something to turn me back into a demon queen."

David snorted. "*Pftt*. You were never a queen—just a Barbie with an oversized head."

Lilith shot him an evil look, but continued. "I knew I needed a powerful energy to transform my mortal body into an immortal one. Necromancers and warlocks are the only ones who can channel such powers. Warlocks and demons have a lot in common. I knew about dark creatures, and I knew where to find the most powerful one. So I dabbled in a little dark magic. With the help of my servants, and after breaking through the first planes of death, I found a specter—and I made a deal with him. I would raise him back from the dead in exchange for transforming me back into a demon."

"Lilith, you don't know what you've done! He's a dark warlock. He can't be trusted."

Lilith's expression darkened. "Right, just like I trusted my own sister."

"You tried to kill me?" protested Kara. "Or have you forgotten that?"

"Ah, the devil is in the details," said Lilith smiling mischievously.

Kara didn't know what Lilith meant. "What—"

"Who says he's going to keep his side of the bargain," interrupted Jenny.

Lilith didn't answer right away. "He will. I'm not worried. Now, enough with the chitchat, let's keep moving."

Kara stole a look behind her. There was no sign of Gideon anywhere.

"Are you hoping for reinforcements?" laughed Lilith. "Forget it. The park is surrounded by dark magic. Even angels can't get through anymore—you got here just in time. Your guardian friends would be foolish to try; their souls would disintegrate into dust. *Poof!*" She mimicked an explosion with her hands and laughed like it was some sick private joke.

Kara ignored Lilith's theatrics. Even if their original plan had failed, there was still hope. Gideon must have a plan of his own. The old witch doctor was clever enough to disappear just at the right time. Or was he just a coward and had abandoned them? Her insides churned.

They passed tall snow banks and snow-covered trees on either side of the path. Slowly they emerged into a large clearing.

Cleopatra's Needle was surrounded by snow covered magnolia and crabapple trees. The obelisk was even bigger than she had first thought. At least seventy feet tall, its sharp granite point stood out like a giant's pencil. Its rough granite surface glowed an eerie green. The six hooded men continued to chant but didn't look up as the group approached.

Kara walked as slowly as she could. She needed time to come up with a rescue plan that didn't involve getting killed. She only needed to fight off the snow beasts, save David and Jenny, and in the process kill all the warlocks, and save the mortal world—no biggy.

She searched for her elemental power. A shimmer came from deep inside her, like a spark of light. It pulsed momentarily, full of promise—and then it went out. It was hopeless. She wished her powers were bottled up in little grenades, like Gideon's. It would be so much easier.

David sensed her discouragement. His smile told her that he didn't want her to feel this was her fault—even if it was her half-sister that started the whole thing. If Kara had finished Lilith off, none of this would be happening. But Kara wasn't like that—she couldn't kill Lilith in cold blood, not even after everything she had done. It wasn't up to her to decide if Lilith lived or died.

Lilith caught Kara and David's tender moment. "Oh, how cute, the ongoing love affair that never goes anywhere," she laughed. "Aren't you two tired of pretending? It's not like I can't *see* the way you're looking at each other. It's so painfully sad. Angels and mortals are a *no—no,* if I remember the rules correctly."

"Shut up, Lilith," hissed Kara. Blood gushed to her face. It was awkward enough having strong feelings for David while she was mortal. She didn't need reminding. David winked and seemed rather pleased with himself. Her face burned even more.

"Oh, look everyone. Look at how red Kara's face is—it's like a tomato," taunted Lilith. "My guess is that your face is so red because you don't want him to know how much you *love* him, am I right?"

Kara's ears burned, and she kept her head down. She didn't dare look at David. If she did, he would see that Lilith was right.

"Leave her alone, albino," said David.

Lilith laughed softly. "Whatever—love is so overrated anyway. It's a disease for the living, for the weak. I don't need *love*—it's a distraction from what is really important."

Kara watched Lilith. There was something odd in the way she said *love*. It almost felt like she was angry. Had something happened to her?

A snow beast came up to Lilith. It brushed its nose against her hip with a pleading look in its eye, like a dog. Lilith smiled and stroked the creature tenderly. It closed its eyes, enjoying the attention. Lilith's face lit up, and Kara saw a kindness in her half-sister that she had never seen before. There was good in her. She saw it.

They were only a few yards away from the obelisk now. Kara's insides twisted at the sight of the men in the black cloaks. Her throat started to close up, and her lungs felt on fire. She took a chance and walked alongside her half-sister.

"Lilith—you don't have to do this." She searched her sister's face.

"You can let us go. You can have a life of your own—you can find love."

"Love? Don't patronize me. I'm not in the mood."

"I know that part of you knows this is wrong. We can help each other. You can come stay with me and my mom after this is finished—you'll love her. We can be sisters, be a family."

Lilith's eyes filled with tears. For a moment, Kara thought she had reached her.

"Stop talking, or I'll cut out your tongue. Move!" Lilith shooed the snow creature away and stormed ahead. She wiped her eyes and clenched her fists.

Kara stared at her half-sister walking away—she even walked more like a girl now and not some demon-diva. Perhaps there was more human in Lilith than she was letting on.

A snow beast prodded her in the back, shaking her out of her thoughts. After stumbling through knee-high snow, the beasts led them right up to the obelisk.

Kara came face to face with the ring of warlocks. The growling creatures retreated, as though they weren't allowed to come any closer.

As she edged nearer, Kara sensed evil that made it difficult for her to breathe, as though cold hands gripped at her throat. Her heart raced, and she felt weak. She stared at the circle of warlocks around the obelisk. She noticed that five of the warlocks' bodies were semitransparent, almost like holograms. Were they specters of lost warlocks? She was sure her fingers would simply pass through their bodies.

But there was one who stood out amongst the others, one whose body was as solid as hers—the dark warlock himself.

A green shadow mist rolled in from the line of trees. It crawled into the clearing and wormed towards the obelisk like a collection of toxic snakes. Kara's heart sunk. Thousands of glowing spheres floated in the mist. It coiled around the obelisk and disappeared into it, taking the souls with it. The obelisk shimmered and expanded as though it were taking a breath.

A hard knot of anger formed in Kara's chest.

A whisper of bells reached her ears. She searched again for Gideon, but there was no sign of the old witch doctor. *Gideon, where are you?*

David and Jenny's saddened faces were illuminated by the thousands of souls that glowed in the mist.

"Kara—we have to stop them," whispered David, as he fidgeted on the spot. "We have to do something."

"I know...I'm thinking," she whispered back.

"Well you better do it fast, because it's starting," Jenny pointed to the sky urgently.

Kara stopped breathing. The sky had turned a deep purple, and the snow had taken on hues of gold. It was as if the park had suddenly been painted. To the west, the orange semi circle of the sun disappeared behind the skyline of Manhattan. Kara glanced at her watch.

4:39 p.m. She was too late.

"You can forget about whatever you were planning," laughed Lilith.

She stared at the obelisk like it was some kind of expensive jewel. "Isn't it beautiful?"

As darkness touched the tip of the obelisk, glowing green runes appeared on its surface. The obelisk became a glowing green totem pole. The ground trembled and moaned. At the foot of the obelisk, a fissure broke the frozen ground and made its way around the warlocks in a perfect circle. Green vapors rose into the air from the ring of open ground.

Bells rang. Kara's pendant burned against her skin. She staggered forward. The one solid hooded figure turned towards her. He stared at her with gleaming red eyes, and she felt invisible bonds strap her wrists. She couldn't move.

You're too late elemental witch, whispered a voice in her mind. *There's no stopping it now. The ritual has already begun. My brothers will rise again—all of you will die!*

CHAPTER 19

THE DARK WARLOCK

KARA WATCHED IN HORROR as five more hooded figures climbed out of the ground. The air was heavy with a mixture of rotten flesh and a hundred year old sewer. Slowly they rose and made their way to stand behind each of the warlock ghosts. Each warlock revenant stood behind a specter. Then they stepped forward into the five specters, which appeared just to have been stand—ins waiting for the real thing. There was a sudden green glow, and then the specters vanished into the cold winter air. The revenant warlocks stood and waited.

The shadow mist disappeared. Kara's heart ached as she watched the last of the souls that had been suspended in the mist disappeared into the obelisk.

"That's it...we've failed," cried Jenny. David rested his hand on her shoulder reassuringly.

But something inside told Kara that this wasn't the end. The ritual wasn't over yet. She stood frozen in the cold, thinking.

She needed a diversion.

Laughter boomed across the park. "Welcome, *friends*," said an echoing voice—the same as the one she had heard coming from the rats.

The dark warlock walked towards them. He was even larger than that big policeman that had showed up at her home. He wore a long black cloak with glowing green circular symbols and runes that shifted like liquid. He stood in front of her and removed his hood.

Kara forgot to breathe. His skin was as rough as leather. It, too, had gleaming green symbols etched into it, as though he had been branded. His red eyes glowed as brightly as sunlight and burned Kara's eyes as she looked at him. Maggots and insects fell from his rotten corpse and left a squirming trail in the snow behind him.

Kara hadn't known what to expect, but she knew right away that he was the same dark warlock that had killed Olga and stolen thousands of human souls. More than anything, she wanted to destroy him.

He smiled, and Kara could see that his blackened teeth were sharpened into fangs like piranhas'. The bonds on her wrists slipped away, and Kara could move again.

"We meet again, elemental witch," he said. "I'm glad you could join us on this very *festive* night."

"Speak for yourself," said David. "There's nothing festive here, *witch man.*"

The dark warlock studied David and Jenny for a moment.

"*Spirit walkers*—we always seem to cross paths, unless I've killed you, of course. I haven't forgotten what your group did to me

228

and my kin. You spirit walkers have always thought yourselves superior to the rest of the supernatural world. You're always meddling in things that don't concern you—crushing down warlocks, witches, and demons. I remember the great war of the warlocks, the battle on Mordent Hill, where we defeated your lot and sent you packing. But then the white witches sided with you spirit walkers and sent me to death. You condemned me to spend my eternal life as a shadow of my past self, to linger forever in nothingness."

"The mortal world doesn't belong to you anymore, spirit walkers. We will destroy all the remaining witches in this world."

He turned his fiery eyes on Kara. "After we finish making some *necessary* changes, we will avenge the blood of our kin. We will take back what was ours."

He lifted his arms in the air. Green flames danced from his fingertips. "Every non-magical being will be our slave. The time of the warlocks has come. We will take the world from the weak. The warlocks will rise to power again."

Hot anger surged through Kara. "It's never going to happen, warlock."

Wergoth edged closer. "You have courage—lots of it. It is no wonder, the elemental power flows so fully in your veins. But it has clouded your judgment, made you cocky. You do not posses the power to stop me, elemental. You and your spirit walker friends will all die tonight."

"No one's dying tonight." Kara stood her ground.

Wergoth's face warped in an evil grin. With a twist of his wrist, his arms blazed with green fire. The five other warlocks arranged themselves behind him. Their long black cloaks trailed behind them, and as they stepped closer Kara could see their rotted flesh beneath their hoods. Their eyes burned with the same evil fire.

In one rapid movement two of the five warlocks lifted their arms, and jets of green fire shot out of their fingers like water from a fire hose. The brute force blew David and Jenny into the air and engulfed their bodies in green fire. They hovered in the air, screaming as the green flames burned their mortal suits.

Without a second thought, Kara ran over to her friends. She reached out to David first, but pulled back her hand in excruciating pain. Her hands were charred and covered with angry red blisters. She tried to ignore the pain and reached out again. But it was like sticking her hands into boiling water, and she could almost feel her skin slipping from her bones. She couldn't touch them.

Jenny's face was contorted in a silent scream. David's body twisted in agony. Their eyes met. She knew he wanted her to run, to leave them here and save herself. But she couldn't. Her eyes burned.

"Stop it! Let them go, you're killing them," she howled.

She looked over to Lilith, but her sister's expression was stone cold.

Wergoth roared in laughter and looked back at his followers.

"Let them go? We will never let them go. Tonight we will drink their souls —and there's nothing you can do, elemental. You were fools to think you could survive a dark warlock's power. We are invincible now. You spirit walkers will fall like flies. And with each fallen soul, we will replenish our strength."

The warlocks stepped forward.

"Stay back!"

Kara narrowed her eyes and made fists with her hands "Don't you touch them! I will kill you!"

The warlocks laughed.

"You know, if you were any smarter, you'd run away and save yourself. Why do you care so much for these spirit walkers? They are worthless."

David and Jenny's cries filled the night as they fought desperately in their green fire prisons. But the more they fought, the more they suffered. Kara knew they couldn't last much longer. She would never give up on her friends—she would fight till the death to save them.

"Gideon, now's the time," she called out to the night sky.

Wergoth's narrowed his eyes. He turned to Lilith. "Where's the witch doctor?"

Lilith paled. Kara saw fear flash in her eyes. "Uh...there was no one else with them, I swear. Just Kara and the other two."

In a frightening rage, the dark warlock lurched forward with lightening speed, like a shimmer of green light, and struck out at Lilith with liquid green fire. Lilith's body lifted into the air and slammed back hard on the ground. She brushed the flames from her coat desperately. Her nice white coat had saved her from being burnt. Shakily, she pushed herself up from the ground. Her blue eyes were wide with fear.

"Idiot!" bellowed the dark warlock. "I sensed the old fool's presence underground—he fought my magic. He was here with them. How could you let him slip from your fingers? I was wrong about you, demon girl—you can't even catch a weak old man."

"I'm sorry...let me go look for him—"

The dark warlock lifted his hand to silence her. "No. I'll deal with him later. We have more important matters to settle. I will not be distracted by that old fool, not when the time is near."

His blazing eyes focused on Kara.

"And now for the human sacrifice," said the dark warlock. He reached into the folds of his robes and withdrew a gleaming sword with green markings etched on the long curved blade. He walked over to Lilith and handed her the sword.

"Kill the elemental."

CHAPTER 20

STARS IN THE SKY

KARA HELD HER BREATH—being sacrificed wasn't part of her plan. The sword gleamed in Lilith's hand. Her own half-sister was going to behead her like Anne Boleyn—except that no one would ever know or care. She was a nobody.

David and Jenny's movements were slowing. Through the green flames Kara could see their angel essence seeping out through their mortal suits. Their souls would soon be destroyed by the fire.

The dark warlock bowed reverently toward the obelisk.

"To make the ritual complete, I need the blood of an innocent, mortal blood. Any mortal blood would do, but I've decided to use *your* blood, elemental."

"Kill her," ordered the warlock.

Lilith hesitated. She looked at Kara. Fear and regret flashed in her tearful eyes, and the silver sword shook in her trembling hands.

"Are you deaf? I said kill her!"

But Lilith didn't move. She opened her mouth to speak, but shut it again. Her lips were shaking. She locked eyes with Kara, and a silent understanding passed between them.

The warlock glared at Lilith. "We need to perform this sacrament *precisely* on the winter solstice—now. It cannot wait. If you don't kill her, then I will!"

The dark warlock drew another sword from under his cloak and advanced towards Kara.

In a flash Lilith lunged at the warlock, her sword high in the air above her head. With force that Kara didn't think Lilith was capable of, she swung her sword at the warlock's head. His body shimmered and disintegrated into a cloud of black mist as though all the molecules in his body had separated.

But the next second, the dark warlock reappeared behind Lilith. He grabbed her from behind and with a great stroke, he slit her throat.

"NO!"

The warlock tossed Lilith's lifeless body to the ground. Her blue eyes stared blankly into the sky.

Kara felt like she was in a dream.

"You...you monster! You promised her. She was helping you! How could you do this?" Rage poured through her like hot magma. Her eyes burned and tears fell freely down her cheeks. Her heart pounded in her ears, and her hatred for him intensified. He was going to pay for this.

The dark warlock laughed. "She was a fool to trust me. Why should you care for someone who wanted you dead anyway. You should be glad, I've done you a favor."

"She didn't deserve to die...not like this." Kara's voice faltered. She had seen good in her half-sister's eyes. It had only been there for a second, but she had seen it. Everyone deserved a second chance. People could change, and Lilith had deserved that chance. But it was too late for her now.

Wergoth brandished his sword. The runes on his skin glowed brighter. "There is nothing more noble than a clean death—you should be so lucky. You should be thankful she died quickly."

He glanced down at Lilith's body, but Kara couldn't tell what he was thinking.

"You're sick. You're a monster. Your place is back in death, and I'm going to send you there for good," Her voice rang out confidently. But what she saw next made her want to scream.

Lilith's blood was flowing towards the obelisk in a thin red stream. It reached the foot of the monument and disappeared under the snow. The obelisk gleamed and shuddered, as though it had accepted the blood as an offering.

Kara felt sick and struggled to keep from falling to her knees. A beam of green light exploded from the top of the obelisk and shone into the night sky.

The warlocks chanted and formed a line in front of the obelisk.

"The ritual is complete—sealed with the blood of the innocent," continued the dark warlock.

He turned to Kara.

"You are unlucky to be here on this winter night, elemental. I cannot let you live—you are too *unpredictable*. The more blood we sacrifice, the stronger our hold on the mortal world will be. The blood of two elementals will be far much more potent than one."

"Wugnor, Wormar, kill her and bring her blood to me," ordered the dark warlock.

The two warlocks separated from the line and surrounded Kara. Green fire danced on their fingers. Their faces were so badly charred by the green runes that she doubted anything human was left in them. Warlock magic held their skin together. There would be no sword fight here. Kara's skills were useless. They were going to burn her to death with their warlock fire.

Kara felt elemental energy surge inside her body. But she needed time to concentrate.

Wugnor attacked, and she charged to meet him. She faked to the left, twirled and landed by Lilith's body. Not chancing a look at her sister's face, she picked up Lilith's sword and sprinted away, just as a shot of green fire exploded where she had stood seconds ago. She was blinded by the smoke, and her lungs burned as she tried to breathe. As she turned, another ball of liquid fire grazed the side of her leg. The heat blistered her skin. She cried out in excruciating pain, as she slapped out the fire with her left hand. She planted her feet, crouched in anticipation and waited.

Wugnor's face twisted into an evil grin. "I haven't had this much fun in centuries. I'm going to enjoy drinking your blood," he said in a high-pitched voice.

He lunged again, rocketing green fireballs at her like a tennis ball machine. Swinging the sword above her head, she hit and diverted the fireballs, using her sword like a baseball bat. She sliced through one fireball after another, splitting them into dancing shards of heat. But she couldn't keep blocking them forever.

Wugnor laughed at her as he moved forward.

Kara saw his mistake. She ducked and twisted away from his shots, rotated her body and slashed an upward stroke cleanly across the warlock's neck. His body fell to the ground beside his head. Kara thought of the headless horseman. Green flames blazed from the body until only dust remained.

The warlock, Wormar, suddenly slashed his warlock fire at her and burned her in the chest. Kara cried out in pain, as she tried to sidestep the killing flames. She felt her energy draining away. Sweat dripped down her back. The sword hung heavily in her hand. She tried to fight the desperation that was poisoning her, but the warlock attacked again and again. He was outmaneuvering her as she desperately concentrated on not getting burned. Sweat dripped into her eyes. Her vision blurred. Kara's strength was fading. The sword slipped from her hand. If only she could call her elemental power—for what good it would do.

Wormar grinned confidently. "Your will to live is admirable, but it won't last, little child."

He stood in front of her with green fireballs poised in his palms and lifted his arms for the killing blow—

Kara ducked, kicked up her sword, caught it, and in the same movement slashed it across his neck. His head bounced at her feet, and green blood spilled from the stub of his neck. His body burned in green flames and then turned to ash.

She heard laughter.

"I'm very impressed by your skills, but you cannot kill us with a mere sword, little elemental," laughed the Dark warlock. "In fact, there is nothing in this world or in the spirit world that can destroy us."

Kara watched the two piles of dust on the white snow. A green glow emanated from them, and then a whirlwind of green glowing ashes rose from the ground. When it dissipated, the two decapitated warlocks stood up with ugly grins on their faces—their heads as good as new. It was going to be harder to kill them than she thought. This sucked, royally.

Wergoth looked to the sky. "We're wasting precious time. I'll kill her, and then we can begin with the other preparations." He raised his arms.

A red bottle shot through the air and hit the Dark warlock in the chest. It exploded and consumed him in a ball of red fire. Kara staggered back, blinded by the light and the heat.

When she opened her eyes, Gideon stood beside her with two more glass bottles in his hands.

"Where have you been?" she said exasperated.

"Hiding," he answered. "Until the time was right."

"Yeah...I noticed." It came as no surprise—the witch doctor had kept himself hidden from the supernatural world for years. She hoped he hadn't waited too long.

"I couldn't risk getting caught, not until I had the time to explain what you needed to know."

Kara didn't have time to ask him what he meant.

The red fire dissipated, and the dark warlock stood unharmed in front of them again.

"Gideon, how good of you to join us," he taunted. "You've saved me the effort of looking for you. I've wanted to kill you years ago, but you always managed to slip away from my grasp. You witch doctors are so devious and cunning—I can never tell what side you're on. All you care about are your pathetic potions and cures. You were never true sorcerers, just outcasts."

"Can't kill what you can't catch," mocked the witch doctor.

The Dark warlock smiled. With a flick of his wrist, he blasted a ball of green fire at the witch doctor. But Gideon was ready. He counterattacked with a bottle of white substance that hit the ball of fire, shattered and enveloped the fire in a ball of white gum-like substance. The fireball plopped to the ground like a giant piece of pre-chewed gum.

Kara used the distraction to examine David and Jenny. They had stopped moving completely, and their eyes were dull and unfocused.

"I need to rescue my friends—"

Gideon held her back. "Not yet."

She wrestled in his grip. "What? Why?"

The other warlocks rejoined Wergoth. Their stench was unbearable. They stood ready and waiting for another onslaught.

Gideon loosened another glass vial on his leather belt and lowered his voice.

"He will come at me with all his power, now. The more he uses, the weaker he becomes. Using magic comes with its price—it's not infinite. He has already wasted most of his powers performing the ritual. After he strikes me down, is when he'll be most vulnerable—he will have had to use most of his powers out to get me—and that is when you must strike him down. If you try before that, it won't work, and you'll die!" said Gideon.

"But, that means...you'll be..." Kara couldn't finish the sentence. Gideon was going to sacrifice himself. "No. I won't let you."

"Don't worry about me dear—I'll be all right. You are the *only* one who can stop them. You don't have a choice—this is what needs to happen. Kara, I need you to focus your powers now. Tap into your emotions and search for the light. Let your light guide you."

It was hard to concentrate, but Kara gave it her best shot. She felt a flicker of power.

"I feel something, but it's not going to be enough..."

"Very good, my dear," Gideon sounded delighted. "Keep working at it."

"But—"

All at once, balls of green liquid fire began to fall from the sky.

Kara jumped out of the way, but the heat scorched her back, and she slammed into the ground.

Gideon was propelled backwards. He landed hard, and Kara heard a horrible crack. But the old man stood up on his shaky legs, his face set.

"Let's see what you got, darkling*s*."

He whipped two bottles at them. In the air, the bottles transformed into a giant orange net. It fell on the warlocks and paralyzed them momentarily.

With a crack, the net melted into an ugly orange soup. The warlocks looked really angry now.

"I've had enough of you, old fool!" The Dark warlock charged, blasting a beam of green fire from his hands.

Gideon threw a handful of yellow powder into the air. It formed a protective wall around him. The warlock's beam of fire bounced back off the wall like a rubber ball and blasted him in his own flames.

Wergoth screamed in rage. He began to chant, raised his arms, and released another powerful blow. Gideon's wall shook, and then it collapsed. As he reached for another bottle, a fiery ball hit him in the chest, and he fell to the ground, his body covered in green flames.

Kara ran over to him. The smell of burnt flesh rose from his badly burned face and hands. His eyes were closed, and she couldn't tell if he was breathing.

"Gideon, please don't be dead." She shook him gently, but he didn't open his eyes. "I need you."

"He was an old fool to think that he could beat me. I am a *dark* warlock, the most powerful sorcerer in this world. He was nothing but a potions master, a soup maker," he laughed. "You can't kill a warlock with seasonings and soup."

"He was more than that—he saved my life. He was my friend," she hissed.

"You're going to pay for this, *warlock*."

A sly smile formed on Wergoth's face. "I'm going to enjoy killing you, elemental. Then I'm going to feast on the souls of your friends." He lashed out.

The force knocked Kara off her feet. She could smell her own hair burning.

Kara stood up, staggering and confused. Crackles of green energy trailed around her. The warlocks' sickening wet laughs sounded all around her.

She glowered at them all. "I'm going to save my friends—and my mother!" she cried.

Wergoth fixed Kara with a look of pure hatred. "No, you're going to die at the hands of warlock fire, a slow painful death."

The dark warlock's skin sizzled with electric power. He raised his hands. "Good bye, elemental."

Before she could react, he hit her with another blast of liquid green fire.

She went crashing down. She cried out in excruciating pain, but managed to roll over and extinguish most of the fire. The flames had scalded her arms and burned through her jacket. She smelled her own burned flesh. She choked as the green vapors burned her lungs like acid. With the last of her courage, she focused on her light. She was just able to push herself back on her feet. Wiping the tears from her eyes, she tried to tap into her power. A pulse started to vibrate through her.

Too late.

Another ball of fire blasted into Kara and knocked her down again. They were going to kill her slowly for fun. She was only just conscious, but she could still hear their sick laughter.

She turned toward Gideon, but he lay exactly as before, no sign of life.

"Gideon, what must I do?" her voice cracked.

Suddenly, the pendant rose from Kara's neck. It hovered for a second, and then it broke free. Soaring through the air like a bullet, it struck the obelisk. It stuck to the structure, as though it were magnetized. Kara watched as the tiny stone began to shine with a brilliant yellow light. It pulsed and swelled like a breathing heart. It stuck there on the obelisk, glowing as if it were trying to tell her something—

And then it came to her, like a tiny voice inside her head. She knew what to do.

She crawled to her feet, trembling. She concentrated on that little piece of light that still lingered inside her. Her light was the key. It was a spark of hope—of life.

She searched deep inside herself, just as she had done many times before as a guardian. She called it forward. Her light pulsed and awakened.

She blinked the blood from her eyes and strained to keep from falling over from exertion. She could feel little tremors beneath her feet, as though the earth herself was responding to her. She stepped forward. Her eyes blazed with rage. She radiated power.

The earth beneath her feet rippled and moaned like an earthquake.

The dark warlock turned towards her, a moment of panic on his face.

Power coursed through her body. And then Kara let her power go.

A bolt of silver lightening shot from her and hit the obelisk. The giant structure lit up as though it were on fire. Kara and the obelisk were connected by a stream of silver light. Her body trembled as the connection held. She strained to empty herself of all of her light, until there was nothing left but an empty core. She exhausted herself—nothing had happened. She stood in the silence for a moment.

Then, with a thundering crack—the obelisk exploded.

Shards of rock and pebbles showered the ground. Where the obelisk had once stood was now a giant gaping hole the size of a garage. The ground began to shake again, and hundreds of glowing green symbols and runes sprouted from the earth and floated into the sky. They glimmered for a moment and then dissolved.

"NO! This cannot be! This cannot be happening! This is impossible!" the dark warlock wailed hopelessly.

Tendrils of silver fire wrapped around the other five warlocks, and bound them tightly in unbreakable chains. The warlocks howled an inhuman sound as the silver flames consumed them. Their bodies bubbled and hissed and finally disintegrated.

The dark warlock screamed as his body, too, was consumed by the silver electricity that coiled around him. He rolled over, howling in pain. A silver glow emanated from his chest and spread slowly all over his body until he was covered in silver light.

"You cannot kill a dark warlock! I AM FOREVER!"

He spat up thick black liquid as he wailed and clawed at his own flesh. He lifted his arms in the air as if he were praying, and then his body crumbled into dust and disappeared in a gust of wind.

Kara drew in a shaky breath as her silver tendrils snaked over the ground around the hole. Like a brilliant tornado, it lifted with it the millions of shattered pieces of the obelisk. In a whirlwind of pebbles and sand, it rose in the air. Piece by piece, the spinning silver energy glued the obelisk back together. When the final stone was back in its place, the whirlwind dissipated. The obelisk gleamed in silver light and cast a moonlight glow over the park. Its runes shone brilliantly for a moment, and then the ancient rock shuddered, and the markings returned to their natural cold grey color.

Kara smiled at the magic. It was beautiful.

And then she collapsed.

CHAPTER 21

SAYING GOODBYE

KARA DREAMED SHE WAS at the edge of the world. Soft puffy clouds covered the horizon, and she was flying towards the sun. This must be how birds felt, and she thought it was amazing.

White light blinded her. When she could see again, she realized she wasn't flying through the sky at all but standing on solid ground in the penthouse on level seven.

The room looked exactly as she remembered, with soft sofas, armchairs, and plush carpets. Twenty-foot high windows ran the length of the room on all four sides, and Kara could see a black sky glinting with stars outside. She blinked through the brightness of the light in the room and felt heat on her face. It was like the luxurious apartment was floating in outer space.

"Hello again, Kara. It's been far too long since we've last seen each other. How have you been?"

Kara turned and gazed into the face of an elderly man. He sat on a large sofa packed with fluffy pillows in the middle of the living room. His round face, pink cheeks, and small sparkling eyes, made

Kara think of Santa Claus—except this one wore a white kimono with gold stars stitched into the fabric, and a golden belt tied around his waist. He looked like he was on his way to a spa.

The Chief cracked open a jar of olives and started to pop them in his mouth one by one.

"Uh...fine, I guess," answered Kara. She couldn't believe how many olives the Chief could put in his mouth all at once—it almost made him look like a grandpa chipmunk.

"I just love olives, don't you?" said the Chief. He dabbed his thick white beard with a cloth.

Kara shrugged. "Not really. I find them too sour, and they always make me think of eyeballs—the ones with the little red parts in the middle."

The Chief raised his bushy brows. "Never thought of them like that. Eyeballs, you say?" Twisting his face, he examined the jar as though it were the first time he'd ever laid eyes on olives before. Satisfied, he placed the jar back on the table.

"Come and sit with me, we have lots to talk about, you and me." The Chief patted the large beige sofa beside him.

Kara walked over and let herself fall into the soft sofa. The coffee table was covered with food and drinks—rice, fried fish, chips, bags of pretzels, a large plate of vegetables and dip, gummy bears, egg rolls, licorice twizzlers, bottles of soft drinks, and a giant bowl of spaghetti and meatballs.

"Would you care for an egg roll?" the Chief grabbed a plate from the coffee table and placed it in front of Kara. "They've gone a little cold, but they're still very tasty. Try one—you'll see."

Kara lifted her hand. "No thanks. I think I'll pass." She was amazed that the Chief could eat all this food. Her eyes went to his large belly, but she knew better not to ask.

"Is my mother safe?" she asked instead, her throat tightening. She had been torturing herself ever since she had left her mother's side. Her last memories of her mother had been horrible.

"Yes, dear. She is perfectly safe—just as are all the other mortals who were infected by the dark warlock's magic. All is well in the world of the living, once again."

Kara sat back relieved. The mission had been a success.

The Chief placed the plate back on the table and grabbed a handful of twizzlers. After tearing a piece off one of them, he waved it like a wand and pointed it at Kara.

"Once again you've surprised us all with your skills, Kara. We are pleased how the events turned out, you know. It was a gamble sending you out to confront a witch and a dark warlock, but I knew you'd pull through. I've always known it—I've been watching you for a long time, and I never stopped believing in you. Besides, you were the only one who had the *necessary* skills to defeat the warlocks."

Kara dropped her gaze. "So you knew about my powers as a mortal all along? I think Ariel knew that my elemental powers would surface. But why didn't she tell me?"

Kara felt her temper rise and tried to keep her expression neutral. Had she been a pawn in the plan all along?

The Chief tore off another piece of his twizzler with his teeth. "We weren't sure *how* they would materialize—or if they were going

248

to show up at all. It was risky. The truth of the matter, Kara, is that we weren't sure it was going to work, but it was a chance we needed to take. We weren't sure of the consequences at the time." He waved a twizzler at Kara. "Twizzler?"

"No thanks."

The Chief studied Kara for a moment. "Kara, do you feel different from before?"

Kara shook her head. "No—should I?"

"When you willingly sacrificed yourself by pouring out the last of your power—when you gave your life wholeheartedly to save the mortal world—that sacrifice changed you."

"Different how?" asked Kara cautiously.

"You are no longer *elemental*."

Kara felt a sting in her chest. For a moment she just sat there, stunned. "What? But...but how can that be? I thought it was a part of me? Being elemental made me who I am? I thought it was like my third arm or something?"

"When you channeled every last bit of your elemental power into that obelisk," said the Chief carefully, "—every *last* drop, so to speak, well, it killed you."

"I figured that much." Kara frowned. "So I'm dead."

The Chief popped open a can of soda and gulped it down in one great sip. He wiped his mouth with the back of his hand. "Not entirely. You drained your elemental part away—that part is gone for good."

"I don't understand? How can I not be *entirely* dead?"

The old man's eyes sparkled, and he smiled. "Just by being alive again, my dear. You will live a normal life, just like any normal mortal girl. You will have your life back."

Kara shook her head, mystified. "So, I'm not elemental...but am I still a guardian angel?"

The Chief waved another twizzler dismissively. "We won't be requesting your services for quite sometime, so the answer is *no*— for now."

"So I won't have any more demons trying to steal my soul, right? They'll leave me alone now, since I'll be *normal*...right?"

"That's what I said."

At first Kara wasn't sure how to feel. She had been a GA with a special ability for more than a year. She had been unique, special, and even though she had been hated by most of the other guardians, she had always secretly enjoyed being different. It had been a big part of who she was—it was what made her special. And now it was gone. But Kara wasn't sad. She was happy.

"So I won't be able to see my friends again? When they're guardians, and I'm not, I mean? I won't see the supernatural anymore? I won't see through the veil?"

"Yes and no. There are still some perks to being a retired GA—we cannot erase your essence completely."

"And I can have a life with David," she was almost afraid to ask, "—a normal teenage life?" It was too good to be true.

"That is not for me to decide," said the Chief with a sparkle in his eye and the tiniest of smiles. "Who knows what the stars may bring."

But even in this incredible moment, there was still something that bothered her.

"I know this might sound ungrateful or selfish, but may I ask you for a favor?"

The Chief smiled. "Of course, Kara dear, anything at all."

"It's about my sister, Lilith. I know she's done terrible things, but she changed—she tried to save me before she died. I believe people can change and deserve a second chance. She's dead now, killed by the warlock, and her body is just lying in the snow. It feels...wrong. She deserves better—even her." Kara strained to compose herself.

The Chief smiled warmly. "You never cease to amaze me, Kara. But don't worry about her, she'll be looked after, I can promise you that." He popped a handful of gummy bears in his mouth. "It is almost time."

Kara screwed up her face. "Huh? Time for what?"

"I'm granting you ten minutes to say goodbye to your friends, and then when you wake up tomorrow morning, things will be back to normal, so to speak. You will not remember any of this."

Kara felt like she was forgetting something. "Wait a minute. What about all the souls?"

"The souls are fine."

"But they're trapped inside the obelisk—"

The Chief lifted his hands to silence her.

"And now my dear, you must wake."

When Kara opened her eyes, she was outside, and David was staring down at her.

"I've never been happier to see those big brown eyes," he said. "Welcome back to the world of the living—"

"—and the dead," interrupted Jenny. Her purple hair reflected in the light behind David.

"Spirit walkers," Jenny laughed, "I'm actually starting to like the sound of that—maybe those witches weren't so bad after all."

Kara smiled. "Maybe they weren't. Maybe they were just...different."

Besides having a jumbo migraine, Kara felt fine. She let David pull her up to her feet. The ground wavered for a second—and then she felt an emptiness, like something was missing, like when you know you've forgotten something, but you just can't put your finger on it. Something was different.

Kara turned her palms over and examined her hands. She wasn't sure what she would find— perhaps some remnant of her power. Her hands didn't appear to be any different from before, and yet she knew her power was gone. She just knew. Her elemental power was spent, like a dead battery. What the Chief had said was all true.

"Kara, what is it?" asked David seeing Kara's mystified expression. "Why are you staring at your hands?"

As the realization sunk in, she looked up at David and Jenny. "It's gone."

"What's gone?" asked David and Jenny together.

"My power—my elemental power. I used it all...and now it's gone. I'll never be elemental again—I'm normal. The Chief said so."

"*The* Chief?" asked David. "The big Cheese? The head honcho? Mr. VIP himself? No way?"

Kara described her conversation with the Chief.

David and Jenny just looked at her, but they weren't sure what to say.

Jenny was the first to speak, "Are you okay with that? I mean, that was a huge deal for you, wasn't it, being elemental and all? I was always kind of envious of you, you know—having a special power."

Kara laughed. "I wouldn't be envious. It's weird, but I feel amazing, like a huge weight's been lifted off my shoulders."

She focused on David. "I can finally be normal—and maybe have a normal life." Kara and David studied one another, and she knew he had put it together. He smiled, his sky-blue eyes danced playfully.

Jenny pouted. "So you're not a guardian anymore? That sucks. Are you sure?"

"Quite sure."

"And you're happy about that," asked Jenny a little more put out.

"I am. I truly am."

Before Kara could explain further, the ground shook and thousands of brilliant spheres flew up from a gap in the ground. It was like an upside-down waterfall. The black sky was immediately illuminated with thousands of brilliant white spheres. Kara felt as if she had just stepped into space and was staring at a newborn galaxy. The souls hovered for a moment in front of Kara—almost as if they were saying *thank you*—and then they shot up into the dark sky like stars until they disappeared into the night sky. Kara knew the souls were safe.

"Where do you think they're going?" asked Jenny.

Kara breathed in the cool air. "Back to their bodies. They'll be reborn into children—life will continue."

All the pent up emotions that she had stored up since the start of the mission were released with the restoration of the souls to the sky. Hot tears fell down her face. It was over. Finally.

With her heart in her throat, Kara walked over to Lilith's body and kneeled. Her sister's skin was snow-white. She had a serene expression on her face. She didn't look dead—she looked like Sleeping Beauty, so calm and peaceful. Carefully, Kara untied the leather bracelet from around her own wrist and tied it gently around Lilith's left wrist. As she folded her sister's hands on her chest, she noticed that her skin was ice-cold and had started to turn grey.

"It's brought me luck, now it's yours. May it bring you luck wherever you go." She bent over and kissed her sister's forehead.

Kara leaned back, and Lilith's body glowed with brilliant particles, as though it had been painted in diamonds. Kara covered her eyes and watched as her sister's soul lifted in the air and disappeared into the sky. And when Kara looked down again, Lilith's body had vanished.

"Can someone help me up?"

Kara turned to see a battered yet very alive Gideon. She rushed to his side and squeezed the old man in a tight embrace.

"You're choking me girl! Let me go. Let me go." His face was blackened, and his hair was still smoking. He looked like a blown out candle.

Beaming, Kara let him go. "I thought you were dead! I thought the warlock killed you."

After wiping himself down, Gideon stood tall and proud. "Tut—takes more than warlock magic to kill old Gideon. I'm a witch doctor." He smiled, and Kara knew there was more to Gideon than he let on.

David smacked Gideon on the back. "Never thought I'd be pleased to see you and your dead pets again, grandpa." He poked the dead fox's glass eye with his finger and jumped back when he saw Gideon's angry face.

"I see all is well, then," Gideon's smile returned. "I said ya could do it. And ya did, Kara, you really did."

Kara felt the blood rush to her face. "Well, I couldn't have done it without you."

Jenny stood beside her, as Kara held out her hand. "Thank you Gideon, for helping us. Truce?"

She waited as if she thought Gideon might take a swing at her.

At first, Gideon just glared at her. And then his expression softened, and he shook her hand.

"Didn't think I'd ever shake hands with the dead. I must be going crazy in my old age."

He looked at Jenny and David. "But I'm happy to know Kara has such good friends looking out for her, even if ya are *spirit walkers*."

Jenny and David laughed. Kara was amazed that the witch doctor had warmed to her spirit friends.

A reflected yellow light in the snow caught Kara's eye. She knelt down and pulled out Olga's pendant. It looked brand new, exactly like the first time she had seen it. She held it in her palm and thanked it silently.

"Look who's decided to join the party," announced David.

Ashley and her team strolled into view. Ashley's expression soured when she saw Kara. She crossed her arms. "What's going on here? You're supposed to be on a mission, not a stroll in the park. Where is the warlock? Did you let him go?" she laughed cynically, and her team followed her example.

"No, he's dead," said Kara cheerfully. "I killed him—and the other ones. The warlocks are all dead. They won't be bothering the legion anymore."

Ashley's expression crumbled.

Kara met Ashley's glare. "I guess we didn't need your *backup* after all. The mission was a success—without you."

Kara paused for a second and then continued, "You tried to make me feel bad about being different. You wanted me to fail and to feel like a freak so you could laugh at me, didn't you? You wanted to turn the legion against me." Kara sneered. "So who's laughing now?"

"I am," laughed David. He pointed to Ashley and her team and began laughing like a lunatic.

Ashley lowered her eyes. "Who is this?" She pointed at Gideon, who jumped back in surprise. "Using mortals to do your bidding is a capital offense. I will have to report you." Ashley's cold smile returned. "Ariel will be very angry with you—you won't be in her good favor for long."

Kara laughed softly. "That's Gideon, a witch doctor—and my friend. And you can write up a ginormous report on me all you want. Why don't you run along and tell Ariel that we didn't need you after all—that she had made the *right* decision in sending me and my friends on this mission—and not you."

Ashley spun around and stormed out the park without another word, her minions following her like sheep.

Kara shook her head and laughed. "Listen, guys. I only have a few minutes left before I—"

"Disappear on us again," said David. "Thought that might happen again."

"Well, I'm looking forward to a normal life for a change," said Kara. She held up the witch's pendant. "Gideon, take this. I can't keep it. I'm sure Olga would want you to have it."

The witch doctor's eyes brightened, and he took the pendant carefully in his large hands.

He beamed. "I would have loved to see that old bat one more time, but I guess we'll see each other soon in another life." He pulled the pendant over his smoking black afro.

"Goodbye, Gideon, and thank you."

"It was a pleasure," said the witch doctor, and he bowed.

Kara turned and hugged Jenny. "I'll see you again—I'm sure of it. This isn't really good bye you know."

Jenny stepped back. "I know. You deserve a normal life Kara—for a little while at least," she winked.

"We have to get going soon, too," said David. "We've been in our M-suits for a long time."

"He's right. And I'm anxious to know how Peter is doing," said Jenny.

Kara felt a cool flutter pass through her like a shiver. She looked down at herself. Her body was becoming transparent, like a ghost.

"It's happening." She trembled with excitement and happiness. She couldn't wait to see her mom healthy and safe, and to start her new life with David.

"Say hi to Peter for me, and tell him I'll miss him."

"We will," said Jenny, despite her smile her eyes were sad.

David laced his fingers with Kara's. "I'll see you soon, my little witch. You can cast a spell on me anytime."

As she held her friends' gazes one last time, she felt David squeeze her fingers. Then she vanished.

CHAPTER 22

FULL CIRCLE

THE PEOPLE ON THE streets were starting to annoy Kara. She narrowly missed a head-on collision with a man with a face like a horse. She spun around, doing a three-sixty as she ran along the street. Sweat trickled down her forehead. As she swiveled sideways, jumped onto the sidewalk and shot through the oncoming crowd, she balanced her portfolio and thought about her big presentation.

She'd hardly slept for the past few days. She'd been too freaked out. She had even skipped her breakfast—since anything going down might come right back out.

Today was her interview with *Ubisoft*, the giant video game design company. Her future was in their hands, and she felt like a total spaz. She had been practicing her speech for weeks and had carefully arranged her portfolio with her best 3d model renderings. But now her brain was numb, as though someone had pressed the delete button and erased her mind.

She pressed her cell phone against her ear. "Okay—I just got onto Saint Joseph Street, so I'll be there like in two minutes."

"Well, you better hurry," said the voice on the line. "I can see a line forming inside, and I think they've already started some interviews. Hurry up, or you'll be late."

"I'm *not* late! I still have ten minutes before my interview. I'm almost there."

A laugh came through the speaker. "I'm just saying—this is supposed to be the most important day of your life—and you're late. You've been talking about this for weeks."

Kara dashed along the busy street. "Excuse me! Coming through—coming through—super important presentation coming through—"

Breathing hard, she squeezed herself through the crowd. She nearly tripped on something and cursed, she couldn't afford to fall down right now. Her heart was in her throat, and her lungs were raw from running. If she were late, she'd never forgive herself. As it was, she would arrive red-faced and sweaty like a pig—a great first impression.

"Okay, I can see you now," said Kara.

David was leaning against Ubisoft's front brick exterior. He wore his favorite brown leather jacket with the collar rolled up, and his blond hair sparkled like gold in the sunlight. He looked like a mix between a young James Bond and Han Solo from *Star Wars*. Their eyes met, and her heart did a somersault. Even after dating for the last few months, he still had that effect on her. Every time she saw him, she felt weak in the knees. She felt as though they had been together for years—it just felt natural to be with him.

"I thought we might catch a bite to eat after your interview," said David through the speaker.

Her cheeks burned. "Let's see how the presentation goes first. I might want to jump into the Saint Laurence River if it goes badly. God, I hope it goes well—"

"Stop worrying. It won't go bad—you'll get the scholarship I'm sure of it. If I can get a scholarship for Mechanical Engineering, there's no way you won't get hired. Besides, I feel like it's going to be a good day."

"I hope you're right."

Kara took a deep breath and sprinted onto Saint Laurence Boulevard. As she ran, her cell phone slipped out of her hand and hit the ground with a crash.

"*Urgh*, I'm such a klutz!" She crouched down to grab her phone.

A flicker of movement appeared in the corner of her eye.

"WATCH OUT!" Someone shouted. She stood up and turned around.

A city bus hurtled towards her.

Kara watched in horror as a city bus came charging straight at her.

She closed her eyes and braced herself for impact—

But the impact never came.

Someone grasped her left arm and lifted her off the ground. She floated in the air momentarily as someone pulled her away from the bus. Her portfolio flew out of her hand, and she landed a few feet away. The bus skidded to a stop and ploughed through the spot where she had stood moments before.

A hand was still wrapped tightly around her arm, and Kara turned around to get a glimpse of her savior.

"Careful there," said a smiling girl with short purple hair and the most dazzling green eyes that Kara had ever seen. She looked like a fairy soldier in a purple bomber jacket with matching purple combat boots.

A shy looking teen boy with glasses and dressed in the same military style helped Kara to steady herself, "Yeah, you don't want to be late for your big day," he said.

Kara's pulse raced. "Huh? How did you know...?" She stared at the pair of them. It took her a moment to compose herself. They both looked strangely familiar.

"Thank you—you saved my life."

"No problem—it's all part of the job," said the girl cheerfully. She shared a look with her friend.

Kara couldn't take her eyes off the two strangers. It was the strangest thing, but she felt like she already knew them. Even their voices sounded familiar to her ears.

"You guys look familiar—have we met before? Did we share a class or something?"

"Or something," said the girl. Her green eyes glistened playfully in the sun.

"So we *have* met before?"

"In another life, perhaps," answered the boy. "But not yet in this lifetime."

"Uh...you've completely lost me. What does that mean?" Kara scrutinized the two of them. Their smiling eyes gave them away. She could tell they were holding something back.

"KARA!"

David tackled Kara in a hug. He squished the air from her lungs and then released her. "Are you all right? You almost got hit by that bus! What were you thinking—crossing without looking?"

Kara felt stupid for being such a klutz. "I know. I know. I was too absorbed with my presentation. I should have been more careful. But I'm fine—thanks to them."

She turned to introduce David to her two rescuers.

"This is David, my..." Kara faltered. They had never really talked about it. She felt his eyes on her, but she couldn't look at him.

"...boyfriend," finished David. He stepped forward and shook their hands. "I'm her boyfriend."

Kara's heart did a jumbo pirouette, and she forgot to breathe. She must have looked astonished because the girl with the purple hair giggled. Kara couldn't help but laugh, too.

"Take care of yourself," said the girl. "Until we meet again. Good luck."

And before Kara could reply, they turned on their heels and walked away. She stared after them until they disappeared into the crowd. She felt sad to see them go—there was something about those two that she just couldn't figure out.

"You dropped this." David picked up her portfolio, which miraculously wasn't damaged. "Someone's definitely watching over you. You could have been killed today, silly girl."

Strangely enough, Kara felt the same way. She couldn't describe it, but she did feel that something or someone was watching over her. Were those two people involved somehow?

But today was going to be a good day; she felt it in her bones. David had just announced to the world that they were an *item*, and she took courage from that. She was ready to face anything.

David held out his hand. "Ready, hot stuff?" His eyes sparkled like the sea.

Kara smiled warmly and interlaced her fingers with his.

She squeezed his hand. "Ready."

Kara took a deep breath. They crossed the street together and disappeared through Ubisoft's front doors.

And now a sneak peek at the next book in the

Soul Guardians series

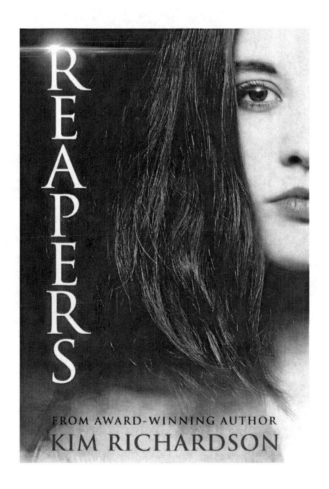

CHAPTER 1

THE DECEPTION

THE SKY OUTSIDE THE bookstore was blood-red. The hot air was thick with electricity, the kind right before a thunderstorm, and yet there were no storm clouds.

Kara moved from the window and pushed off with one foot. The rolling library ladder sped across the wood floors, which creaked and popped under her weight like the rumbling of thunder. Using the ladder was her favorite chore in the bookstore. She loved the way it made her feel like she was almost flying. If only she had *wings*. She could fly up to the highest bookshelf without a ladder and get her work done faster. The sooner it was done, the sooner she could be with David.

She missed him. She missed his voice, his sense humor, and even his arrogance. Yes, he was insufferable at times, but she could never stay angry with him for long. He would always make her laugh in the end, no matter how much she wanted to punch him in the face. It was in those moments in his company that she came alive. When they were together, she could be herself. It just felt right. They fit.

The ladder skidded gently to a stop against a large bookshelf at the other end of the store.

"I'll never understand why he puts the cinematography books so high," she said, exasperated.

With the book *It's only a movie: Alfred Hitchcock, A Personal Biography* between her teeth, she climbed to the top. She leaned out from the side of the ladder, suspending herself dangerously from one foot, stretched out as far as she could, and squeezed the book between *The Making of Psycho* and *The Stanley Kubrick Archives*.

"One of these days you're going to fall and break your neck," warned Mr. Patterson as he polished a crystal ball the size of a grapefruit.

Instead of his usual colorful Hawaiian shirt and Bermuda shorts, he wore a brown plaid suit with a red bowtie that looked like it had been in the back of his closet since the 1970s. Kara could smell the mothball stench from the top of the ladder. She wrinkled her nose and tried hard to keep a straight face. His thin white hair was combed over awkwardly, as though he had dressed in the dark. The only things that were not so out of place were his bare feet. They poked from under his pants as usual. Her boss never wore any shoes.

Kara bit her lip and tried hard not to laugh. He had obviously made an effort to make himself somewhat presentable. But why?

Maybe Mr. Patterson had a date later? Could there be a potential Mrs. Patterson in their midst? But that didn't make any sense. During all the months she'd been helping him out at the bookstore, he had never mentioned any female friends. Then again, he had never mentioned *any* friends. She always thought of him as a loner, stuck in his old ways, like many older folks. He kept to his shop.

"Don't worry," said Kara after a moment, "No one's going to die today."

"You say it like you know for sure, but you don't."

Mr. Patterson spit on his crystal and rubbed it gently, eyeballing it like it was a large precious diamond.

"Mortals cannot foresee the future. They don't have the *acquired* skill and gift that is *foresight*. Only oracles—"

He caught himself and peered over at Kara through his bushy white eyebrows. He watched her as though he had said too much, as though he had revealed some great secret.

Kara watched him with increased interest. It wasn't the first time she had heard Mr. Patterson refer to himself as an *oracle*, whatever that was. She had gotten used to the way he sometimes spoke in the third person. It was almost as though he had a secret identity and lived two different lives, like a spy.

It was a ridiculous notion of course. He was just old and a little confused. Most likely, his identity crisis was the result of spending night and day reading books about clairvoyants and the great beyond. He was obsessed with anything *supernatural*. Maybe he perceived himself as a connoisseur of the paranormal, a modern-day Ghostbuster.

Kara smiled. She cared deeply for the man. He was like the grandfather she had never known, and he felt like family to her.

But there was something different in the way he had just looked at her, as if he had gone too far this time and had said too much and wished he could take it back.

Mr. Patterson frowned and avoided her eyes. He mumbled angrily to himself as he buffed the crystal ball so vigorously that he looked as if he were trying to light a fire.

"Keep her safe," Kara heard the old man say. "That's all I have to do. Well, easier said than done. Thank you very much. If only they knew…"

Kara laughed uncomfortably. "Don't worry, nothing will happen to me. I know what I'm doing. It's just a ladder, no harm done."

"You kids these days," said Mr. Patterson. Kara could see sweat on his forehead. "Always living on the edge, always looking for new ways to hurt yourselves. Tell me, why is that? Why are you all in such a hurry to kill yourselves?"

"I don't know," answered Kara as she slid down the ladder and landed with a thud. "Guess we feel our lives are *boring*. Maybe we're looking for some adventure to spice things up a bit. Weren't you ever young? Don't you remember what it was like?"

"You think your life is *boring*?" Mr. Patterson looked up from his crystal ball.

Kara shrugged. "I don't know…maybe."

She looked into Mr. Patterson's blue eyes.

"Didn't you ever get the feeling that something was missing in your life? That strange empty feeling, like you're supposed to be doing something, but you just don't know what it is? Sometimes, well actually all the time, I get this weird feeling that I was *meant* for something greater—like I have a purpose in life, but I just can't figure out what it is. Not yet, I guess. You know what I mean?"

Mr. Patterson stopped polishing his crystal and watched Kara with his mouth slightly open. He looked worried, like she had discovered some dark secret. He frowned and watched her without blinking. Kara could see fear flicker in his eyes, as if he knew that something bad was going to happen to her.

Kara squirmed uncomfortably under his stare.

"Uh…so…what are you all dressed up for?" she looked away, hoping to change the subject quickly before Mr. Patterson burned a hole in her forehead with his laser-beam eyes.

"Do you have a date or something?"

Mr. Patterson looked at Kara for a while before he answered.

"Of course not. Don't be ridiculous." He waddled over behind the counter and placed his crystal carefully inside a glass case. "It's the annual Festival of Spoken Word at The Couch café. I've been invited to read my poetry—"

"You write poetry?" Kara smiled, glad not to be the center of attention anymore. "I never knew that. That's awesome. Something tells me that you're a fantastic writer. Can you read me some?"

"No."

"Why not?"

"Because."

"Because why?"

"Because *I said so*, and don't try to change the subject."

Mr. Patterson looked at Kara with such intensity that it forced her to look away.

"What did you mean by saying you *feel* that you have some sort of greater purpose in life?" he pressed. "What exactly is this *feeling*? Can you tell me more about it? Can you describe it?"

Kara shrugged. She wasn't sure why her boss would be so interested in that. Didn't everyone feel like their lives were empty at some point? She was sure she'd read that somewhere.

"I don't know how to describe it. It's just a feeling I get sometimes. It's just like I said."

"Humor me."

Kara exhaled heavily, a little annoyed by Mr. Patterson's strange questions and peculiar behavior. She pursed her lips and contemplated how best to explain her feelings so that he would be satisfied once and for all.

"It's like," began Kara, "it feels like...like that feeling when you've forgotten something, or someone's name, and you just *can't* remember what it is. It's kinda like that. Like I'm supposed to be doing something, and I just can't remember what - but I *know* it's something *important*. And it's always there with me, in the back of my mind, and I just can't figure out what it is."

Kara looked directly at Mr. Patterson.

"It feels like I'm about to see a glimpse of my destiny, but then it fades away. To tell you the truth, it's getting to be really annoying. I just wish I knew what I'm supposed to know or remember."

Mr. Patterson looked troubled.

"What? Why are you looking at me like that? What did I say?"

Mr. Patterson pressed his fingers on the counter. "And you get these *feelings* often, you say?"

He was questioning her as if she were in an interrogation room at the police station, just before she was about to get roughed up. She wished she'd never even mentioned that stupid feeling she got, whatever *it* was.

Kara rubbed her fingerprints off the glass on the counter with the sleeve of her grey cardigan. She didn't look at her boss.

"Why are you interrogating me like I'm a criminal? Did I do something wrong? If not, then I wish you'd stop. It's as if I'm failing some kind of test."

Mr. Patterson leaned forward. His voice was tense.

"You did nothing wrong. But this is *extremely* important."

Kara hesitated. "Why?"

"Because these feelings might mean that you—"

BOOM!

The hairs on the back of her neck stood on end, and Kara turned toward the sound. When she realized she was holding her breath she let it go.

"It came from the window," breathed Kara shakily. She frowned. "I think those delinquents are back again. I'm going to kill them for scaring me like that."

Before she could stop him, Mr. Patterson pulled out the baseball bat he kept hidden behind the counter.

"They're going to answer to me this time!" his voice rumbled with rage, and for a moment Kara was glad he had temporarily forgotten about her strange feelings. That interrogation had been awkward enough for an entire month.

As Mr. Patterson moved from the counter, his bat swinging above his head, Kara grabbed his elbow and steered him away.

"Let me check first," she said.

She lowered his bat with her hand.

"I think clobbering kids to death with a bat is a capital offense. We don't want you to murder anyone just yet," she laughed. "You have a poetry reading tonight, remember? Let's focus on that, shall we? This is just a classic case of child boredom."

She pointed a finger at him. "You wait here."

Kara made her way across the room, bracing herself before telling off the ten-year-old boys who had been vandalizing the stores along the street since the beginning of the summer.

"We called the police!" she cried as she stepped out of the front door. Her face had reddened with the sudden rush of blood.

"The police are on their way—"

But there was no one there.

People from across the street stopped and stared at her like she was crazy. She blushed and looked away.

She walked along the front of the store inspecting it for broken glass or any signs of vandalism. But there was nothing. No kids. No broken glass. Nothing.

"That was weird," Kara brushed her hair from her eyes.

And just as she started to walk away, something small and black caught her eye. She turned around and looked back.

Below the bay window was a large black bat. Its neck was twisted awkwardly, and its black leathery wings were limp. It wasn't moving.

Kara rushed over to the bat and gently scooped it up in both hands. With tears in her eyes she pressed on its belly gently, but there was no movement. The bat lay limp in her hands.

"This is bad," came Mr. Patterson's voice behind her.

Kara whirled around.

"I know it's bad. The poor thing is dead. I think its neck is broken. But I don't understand why a bat would be out now in the middle of the day. Don't you think that's weird?"

She paused.

"Okay, what's the matter now?"

Mr. Patterson was eyeing the bat like it was a bomb about to go off.

"It is a bad omen to see a bat in broad daylight, and worse to have one hit the window and die. Day-bats are unnatural. It is a sign that the balance of things has shifted. Something *unnatural* is near— something not from this world has entered."

"I'm *so* confused right now."

"Bats, like birds, are messengers. Something terrible is coming—something dark and evil and not of this world."

Kara had had about enough of Mr. Patterson's strange behavior.

"I think you've been cooped up in this bookstore for too long. I don't get why people are so afraid of bats. I mean they're so cute and smart. Think about how clever they are to use their echolocation to help them find their meals in the dark."

Kara felt sorry for the little creature as she rubbed its fur with her thumb.

"I think a night off reading poetry might do you some good."

She stared at the bat. Its black eyes were half closed. "I'm going to take it to the park and find a place where I can lay it down at peace. It just doesn't feel right to put it in the garbage. It should be with nature."

But just as Kara turned, Mr. Patterson yanked her back.

"No. Leave the bat. I'm telling you—this is *bad*."

He glanced up into the sky like he was expecting something dark to come from the clouds and kill them.

"Ooookkkayyy," said Kara, as she wiggled out of the old man's iron grip. "It's only a dead bat, not the Ebola virus."

She wondered if Mr. Patterson was showing the first signs of dementia. His eyes shone bluer than usual. Was that a sign? She wanted to bury the bat properly, whether or not the old man objected.

Before Mr. Patterson could grab her again, Kara bolted across the street.

"I'll be right back, just give me five minutes!" she called back and headed for Maple Park at the end of the block.

Mr. Patterson's cries echoed in her ears, but she ignored him and ran harder. She needed some space, and the park would give her that. She would find a nice place to lay the bat. It was the least she could do. It did die because of their window.

When she turned around, she caught a glimpse of the old man hurrying after her. His mouth and eyes were wide, but she was too far away to hear what he was saying. As she ran faster she tried not to look at the bat. The more she looked at it, the worse she felt.

She entered the park and slowed to a walk. She searched the grounds for a spot and found a great crabapple tree. Its deep burgundy leaves rustled in the breeze, almost like it was summoning her.

"Perfect."

Kara strolled across the lush green grasses and knelt at the foot of the great tree. Carefully, she nestled the bat between two large gnarled roots that peeked from the earth. It looked like a cradle, and it seemed to be made for the little furry creature.

"There."

She leaned against the tree, satisfied that she had done the right thing.

Kara sat by the tree. She stared at the bat and stared out into space for a long time. The mosquitoes started to bite, and the sky turned a dark blue. She knew she had stayed too long.

Mr. Patterson would probably be furious with her. She had expected him to show up at the park, red-faced and sweating, but he never did. Weird. He seemed so certain that something bad was about to happen. He seemed to believe that whatever it was, it was going to happen to *her.* So why wasn't he here?

She felt guilty. He was old. He couldn't keep up with her seventeen-year-old legs. What if he'd fallen down and seriously hurt himself? She would never forgive herself. She had to get back and check on him.

With a final farewell glance at the bat, Kara pushed herself up. She turned around and almost bumped into someone.

She jumped back in surprise.

"David?" she said.

She pressed her hand on her chest. "You scared me half to death. What are you doing here? I didn't even hear you come. How did you know where I was?"

David watched her, but he said nothing. He was sweating profusely, like he had just run a marathon. His skin was a pale sickly green, and his bottom lip trembled. He looked like he had a fever.

"What's the matter?" said Kara, breathing hard. "You don't look well. Are you feeling okay? David?"

There was something different in the blue of his eyes and his face, like a shadow, but when she focused on him again, it was gone.

David wiped his sweaty forehead with his trembling hand, and Kara noticed a series of deep cuts on his wrists.

"I need you to come with me now."

It was David's voice, but somehow it was also different, almost like a recording of his voice.

Kara shifted uneasily. "Come with you where? David, you don't look well. Maybe we should go to the clinic and see the doctor."

He looked over his shoulder and then surveyed the park before he spoke again.

"You need to come with me," he repeated, and then added gently. "Please, please come with me. Now."

"You're not making any sense," she said gently. "Besides, I can't, right now. Sorry. I need to check on Mr. Patterson. Actually, I need to *apologize* to him if I want to keep my job—"

"Mr. Patterson?" sneered David. His voice was coated with venom, and he watched her intensely.

Kara felt a slow panic begin to stir in her chest.

David turned away from her and kicked the ground.

"Those creatures think they are so very clever. Oracles!" He spat. "The great clairvoyants. The crystal readers." And then he added in a low voice. "Oracles are meddlers."

"Did you say *oracle*?"

Kara didn't remember Mr. Patterson ever speaking about oracles when David was around. In fact she was *certain* of it—as certain as Mr. Patterson had been that the bat was a bad omen.

Kara stepped forward and put her hand gently on David's shoulder. "David, what's the matter? You're not yourself."

David glared at her. His voice rose and his face twisted into an ugly grimace. "Did you forget about our plans? We had made plans tonight. Come on, let's go now."

Kara felt like she'd been punched in the gut. She stared at David.

"I...I don't remember, but I'm sure we did. Why don't we go back together? I just need to pop by the bookstore first—"

"No!" David slapped her hand from his shoulder and laughed nervously.

He wiped his face with his black t-shirt and forced a smile.

"I mean, not yet. We can go later. But first I want you to come with me to the forest," he said. "Come, let's go to the forest."

"David, it's dark. And the forest is even darker. Why do you want to go in there?"

"Don't you trust me?"

Kara felt the beginnings of tears but forced them away. She swallowed hard, and when she spoke her voice cracked.

"Of course, I trust you."

"Then do as I say." He turned to face her. His eyes were bloodshot and crazed. He leaned toward Kara and shouted. "Let's go. Now!"

Kara took a step back. David looked evil. She hardly recognized him.

David noticed the fear on Kara's face and lowered his voice.

"I'm sorry," he said, smiling unnaturally, as though it pained him to do so. "I can see that I'm scaring you. That's not what I wanted."

Kara cringed at the madness in David's eyes.

"What's the matter with you? You sound so different...you sound like someone else."

David smiled cruelly, looking like someone else again.

"Fine. Then I'll go by myself. Don't expect me to be there for you anymore. Without trust you can't have a relationship. There's nothing. I gave you a chance, and you let me down, Kara. It's over."

He turned on his heel and left.

Kara stared back at him, and tears rolled down her cheeks.

David had just broken up with her... But why? Because she didn't want to waltz into the spooky forest—it didn't make sense. She'd never seen him behave like this.

It was over, he had said.

It seemed that David had disappeared. She didn't know who this cruel person was. What had happened to him?

Kara stood frozen in place, hoping that he would change his mind and come back. But he didn't.

She watched David disappear through a line of pine and hemlock trees, and then she started to move toward the forest herself. She was going to give him a piece of her mind. Whatever was wrong, they were going to *talk* about it—

But Kara's blood went cold, and her breath caught in her throat when she saw a dark shape appear where David had stood just seconds before.

The shape was a head taller than David. It moved gracefully between the trees and then disappeared after him through the thick wall of shrubs. Was it a trick of the light? Was the forest playing with her mind? This wasn't just a case of an overexcited imagination. She couldn't explain it, but she just knew it was evil.

It is a bad omen to see a bat in broad daylight. Mr. Patterson's voice sounded in her head. *...It is a sign that the balance of things has shifted, that something unnatural is near—something not from this world has entered.*

Kara was frightened. Mr. Patterson had been right—she wasn't imagining demons again. This *was* real evil, and it was going to kill David.

About the Author

Kim Richardson is the award-winning author of the bestselling SOUL GUARDIANS series. She lives in the eastern part of Canada with her husband, two dogs and a very old cat. She is the author of the SOUL GUARDIANS series, the MYSTICS series, and the DIVIDED REALMS series. Kim's books are available in print editions, and translations are available in over 7 languages.

To learn more about the author, please visit:

Website

www.kimrichardsonbooks.com

Facebook

https://www.facebook.com/KRAuthorPage

Twitter

https://twitter.com/Kim_Richardson

CPSIA information can be obtained at www.ICGtesting.com
Printed in the USA
LVOW10s1558220316

480253LV00002B/264/P